The
Glamorous Life 2

All that Glitters Isn't Gold

Also by Nikki Turner

Project Chick II: What's Done in the Dark

Available as an E-Book

Unique

Unique II: Betrayal

Unique III: Revenge

The
Glamorous Life 2
All that Glitters Isn't Gold

Nikki Turner

 St. Martin's Griffin ♞ New York

THE GLAMOROUS LIFE 2: ALL THAT GLITTERS ISN'T GOLD. Copyright © 2013 by Nikki Turner. All rights reserved. Printed in the United States of America. For information, address St. Martin's Press, 175 Fifth Avenue, New York, N.Y. 10010.

www.stmartins.com

Library of Congress Cataloging-in-Publication Data

Turner, Nikki.
  The glamorous life 2 : all that glitters isn't gold / Nikki Turner.
      p. cm.
  ISBN 978-1-250-00144-3 (pbk.)
  ISBN 978-1-250-03885-2 (e-book)
  1. African American women—Fiction.   2. Businesswomen—Fiction.
3. Rich people—Fiction.   4. City and town life—Fiction.   I. Title.
II. Title: Glamorous life two.
  PS3620.U7659G573 2013
  813'.6—dc23

                                                        2013032949

St. Martin's Griffin books may be purchased for educational, business, or promotional use. For information on bulk purchases, please contact Macmillan Corporate and Premium Sales Department at 1-800-221-7945, extension 5442, or write specialmarkets@macmillan.com.

First Edition: November 2013

P1

This book is dedicated to two men with amazingly impeccable spirits who touched the lives of so many. . . .

Eric "Von Zip" Martin
I know for sure there will never be another like you to walk this Earth. I was blessed to be able to learn so much from you and share a great part of my life with you. Your illuminating personality will be deeply missed.

Matthew Shear
You not only believed in so many of our books but you also gave us opportunities.

Acknowledgments

First all credit and praise must go to the most-high God Almighty. He is the real author of this book. It is *only* through him that I'm able to do this. Without him none of these words would even be possible.

My editor, Monique Patterson, for having so much patience while still maintaining your enthusiasm about this project. Through this hard labor, you were the perfect birthing coach—you always stayed calm, reminding me to breathe when I could see no end. Thank you! Thank you! Thank you!

To the love of my life, my son, Timmond. I'm in awe of the gentleman you are turning into. Always know that you can do anything that your heart desires. Stay focused on your goals because dreams do come true. Kennisha, you have matured so much over such a short time as you have evolved into a lady. Love, laugh, and continue to press forward to your goals.

So many have come and gone through my life, but there are a few permanent fixtures that always remain. My lifelines: Craig, even when I take you for granted, you always remain so consistent with me. I will always love you for that. My brother and best friend, Curtis Chambers,

Acknowledgments

over the years you kept me on my toes, trying your best to keep me foolproof. Tony Rahsaan, you should coin that phrase you are only a phone call away—literally, by the time I hang up with you, my problems are always solved. Bonnie Bling Grier, you have undoubtedly been my lifesaver more times than I can count and I love you for it and I'm so grateful to you.

My lifelong friends: Nikki Gillison and Dame Wayne, you two never disappoint me, always there with your logic and love, only wanting the best for me.

My brothers: Tim Patterson, you always seem to know the right words at the right time. EJ Matthews, you allow me to see things just as they are, even though most of the time I don't want to see it the way you see it, but I take heed. Les Seide, you keep it so real and are always there with the answer I need. Jason Solomon, through our differences you will always be my brother. My cousins: Evan and Latimer, you should have been my brothers. I appreciate you both for your unconditional love. Angela Flunoroy, our talks and laughs really got me through a tough time! Yolanda Chester, I can't tell you how much I appreciated the weekend you came over to cook for me so I could stay focused on my deadline; a small thing to you yet so huge to me. Moyn, what can I say? I honestly appreciate the role you played in my life, while I wrote this book, and through all the craziness you will always have a special place in my heart.

Marc Gerald, after over a decade you still are excited about my new ideas and continue to bring me amazing projects.

Always the best for last: My loyal, die-hard Nikki Turner readers! I'm so humbled by your undying support for my works. You drive me, you inspire me and show me the true meaning of love. I thank you from the bottom of my heart that you continue to allow me to share my stories with you. THANK YOU! THANK YOU! THANK YOU!!!!

Prologue

"Get the fuck out!" Shelly screamed at the top of her lungs, then took another deep breath. "I said, get the fuck outta here." Nobody moved, and then she gave a look that should've intimidated the two little people standing in front of her. When nobody moved, she stressed the word, "Now!"

Fourteen years old, Calliope stood there listening to her mother (in name only, because God knows she didn't act like one) talk to her like a dog. But, hell, a dog got more compassion.

"I said get the fuck out!" Shelly screamed again after not getting the results she wanted the first time. She had that nasty look on her face. The one that said, "Don't make me tell you again."

Compton, only ten, held on to Calliope's leg for dear life. She'd always protected him, and she wouldn't stop now.

With tears in her own eyes, Calliope confronted their mother. "Momma, please don't do this to us. Please," she pleaded not even for herself, but more for her brother. "I'm begging you,

Momma, don't do this to us . . . at least not tonight. Please, Momma." The desperation in her voice intensified with each plea for compassion.

Shelly, who was in fact her biological mother, was unmoved by her daughter's pleas. With no kind of remorse at all, Shelly firmly said with the nastiest demeanor, sucking her teeth so hard that she spat the words out like a spoonful of shit she was trying to purge from her mouth, "What the *fuck* I tell you about begging a motha-fucka to do shit for you?" She snapped her neck and added, "And that includes me. Now"—cold eyes, as intense and lethal as deadly lasers, stared back into Calliope's eyes—"now, lil' girl, get the fuck outta here."

Incendiary words, as damaging—if not more so—as a runaway meteor crashing into a metropolitan city.

But Calliope's feet were Gorilla Glued to the old carpet, and she stood her ground. Face-to-face with her mother, she couldn't move. She stared into Shelly's face, thinking a few choice words: *Why are you such a bitch, Momma? We're your flesh and blood and you treat us worse than dirt. Is it because you're lonely and thirsty for a man's attention? Or are you just a mean nasty bitch by nature? I can fend for myself,* she wanted to say, *but Compton is only ten. I don't need your love. But he does.* All those things she wanted to say, but she didn't. As she always had in the past, Calliope bit her tongue.

Unable to comprehend why his mother would put him out in the cold in the middle of the night, Compton started crying, not wanting to go anywhere.

"Shut up, you lil' faggot! Crying is for the weak," Shelly said to her son. "And I don't raise no weak-ass, pussy-ass, faggot-ass niggas. Matter fact, I should give your sorry ass something to cry for." She raised her hand up in a striking pose as if she was going to hit him, but before she could follow through with the threat the trill of the ringing of a phone snatched her attention and stopped her in motion. With one hand on her hip and the other pointed at Compton, Shelly said, with a deep passion, "That crying shit is for pussies! And I should beat the shit out yo lil' ass fo' crying," but Compton ignored her and bawled even louder.

The worst part wasn't getting put out in the rain. Calliope had grown used to her mother's whimsical bullshit. Numb by it all, she realized at a young age (younger than Compton even) that life wasn't fair, and her mother damn sure didn't play fair. But it cut Calliope all the way down to the marrow in her bones to see her brother cry this way, a way that she would never get used to.

Unable to stop it before, Calliope had witnessed firsthand her mother whip Compton unmercifully until she got tired of swinging the belt for things so small as him dropping a piece of noodle on the floor. At times Calliope even jumped in front of the belt, and it was brutal. That was something that Calliope didn't want to happen to him again. The thoughts of such uncalled-for brutality toward an innocent child compelled Calliope to bend to her brother's height and comfort him with a hug.

Shelly put a hand on one hip and pointed with the other and said, "You best shut that lil' motherfucka up and do what the fuck I say before I put my foot up you and that lil' fucka asses." She reached for the phone, and the look she lobbed in their direction was more effective than a live grenade in a field of battle. Immediately Compton swallowed his cries, but the poor child's tears still poured down his dispirited face uncontrollably.

Wrapping her arms around him was all that was left for Calliope to offer for comfort for her brother. The embrace felt good, and she prayed that it felt as good to him as it did to her. After the hug she took her brother by the hand and slowly led the way out of the house, onto the long covered back porch.

The porch stretched the width of the house, encased by a rickety screen and a roof that had no chance of keeping the rain off them.

This wasn't the first time that Shelly had made them sleep outside on the back porch (sometimes it was kind of fun), but this was the first time that it was pouring down rain, thunderstorming, and flashing lightning, with the weatherman and every citizen of Miami, Florida, anticipating a hurricane.

A few minutes passed with Calliope and Compton sitting on the porch, hoping that their mother, or Mother Nature, would somehow have a change of heart.

Then, through the pregnant raindrops whistling and whipping every which way, Calliope saw a big, red, shiny long Cadi bend the corner and park in front of the house.

The Cadi belonged to Big Jack, her mother's current boyfriend, and he hated kids.

Reality set in; she knew they were really going to be out back, figuratively as well as literally. She thought about what kind of man or human would allow a woman to put her two kids out of the house.

A selfish-ass nigga with control issues, she concluded. One that when she got older, she would positively not tolerate in her life.

Inside, Shelly opened the door for Big Jack with a wide co-quettish smile and wearing a tight red dress. "I thought you wasn't going to make it—with the weather and all." She graciously accepted the brown paper bag Big Jack offered her—an open bottle of Hennessy, her favorite Cognac.

She was brick-house thick and her hair was long, black, and naturally curly, and she had a complexion that resembled raw gold. Shelly wasn't always so needy for a man. In high school she could've had any guy she wanted. But she only had eyes for a new guy who transferred in from California, Compton Sr., who revolved in and out of her life but was her children's father, and who she thought was her soul mate.

Silly Shelly.

Too bad that saying that everybody plays a fool, no exceptions to the rule, was true.

He left her with two kids and a ran-down house with major repairs that he promised to fix, but it was now barely worth half of what she had paid for it. At least she still had her Coke bottle figure though, and she thanked God every day for that.

All she ever wanted and dreamed of was to be loved and rescued by a decent man. And most men, the ones she met anyway, weren't in the business of raising another lion's litter. That, especially, was the case with Big Jack. Though he had paid for a babysitter for tonight, he hated kids and made it clear that he wanted them out of sight. Shelly had used the money to help get her hair, nails, and lingerie tight. Big Jack wasn't going to make some jacked-up bitch his wife, she reasoned with herself. So she had to get creative when it came to finding a place for the kids to stay.

A handful of her left cheek in his right palm, her butt cozying between his cupped fingers, Big Jack gave her that satisfied smile, the one that promised that, if only for tonight, he was her man.

The rain poured from a pitch-black sky, and Calliope knew she couldn't worry about Big Jack or Shelly. The only things on her mind were survival and keeping her and her little brother safe and out of the storm.

Trees were bending to their limits, looked like they would be uprooted under the strong, penetrating force of the wind. Clutching Compton's hand, she said, "We're gonna have to make a run for it," meaning the outhouse.

The shed in back of the house was old and dark but constructed with cement blocks, so structurally it was safer than the dilapidated wooden porch they were on.

"B-But snakes in there," Compton stammered.

Just because she'd never seen any snakes in the shed, personally, didn't mean Compton wasn't right in his assumption.

"You are bigger than any little ol' snake," she told him. "It's going to be a lot safer in there than out here in this storm. Besides, there are going to be snakes that walk on two legs in this world." Though she was only a month shy of her fifteenth birthday, Calliope had seen a lot. "We can't be scared of them.

We just gotta prepare ourselves the best way to deal with and protect ourselves from them."

Compton was slow taking in the jewel his sister had given him because he was too preoccupied with the storm. He watched in awe as the trees jerk danced to the music of the ferocious wind and buckets of water fell from the sky. "Do you think the wind will blow it away?" He meant the shed, not the trees. Calliope didn't know the answer.

"I don't think so," she said honestly. "But I do know that as long as we're together, nothing in this world can blow us apart from each other." Lightning struck, illuminating the sky, then the rain started coming down even harder. Though she wanted and tried to be as tough as she could, the hard-hitting hail coming down on the roof of the porch made Calliope scared as hell herself. She was sure that the possibilities of the porch caving in were very high and knew they had to move, because when it did collapse, the very place where they did not want to be was under that awning. She said to her brother, "Okay. I need you to be a big boy and to run as fast as you can."

He sucked in air, poking out his chest, and said, "Okay. Don't worry, I'm not scared. Super Compton will protect you from dem snakes," he boasted, ready to run, ready for whatever, as long as he was with his sister. "Super Compton is ready for takeoff."

The siblings streaked across the lawn like two bolts of lightning. Both reached the ancient shed at the same time, milliseconds before an actual jiggered sphere of electricity lit up the blackened Miami sky. Immediately following the light show, a clap of thunder shook the ground. Calliope, still holding tight to Compton's hand, asked, "Are you okay?"

He nearly jumped out of his tennis shoes. "I'm f-fine," he said, but he was still shaking.

The shed had been there long before they'd moved in to the small Monopoly-style house, before either child was a thought, even before Shelly was born.

It was dark, no lights, and had a strong mildew smell. Besides that, the shed wasn't too bad. Even so, Calliope wanted to burst out in tears, but thought better of it. There was no need to—what was crying going to do? What was it going to solve? Absolutely . . . nothing! She had learned a long time ago that crying wouldn't get any results. Besides, the sky was crying enough for everyone that night.

The cold and their soaking wet clothes didn't help at all. Luckily, there was an old blanket they could use to wrap up in. It had previously been used to cover up an antique-looking dresser. But at that moment they needed it more than any piece of furniture did. Although the comforter smelled horrible, they were warmer than they'd been before, so they would tolerate the foul odor.

While they waited for the storm to burn out, Compton fell asleep in Calliope's arms, but she stayed awake thinking how messed up their life was and how when she had kids she'd never do anything like this to her children. She'd only fill their life with lots of love. As she sat there watching her brother sleep so peacefully, all that was left for her was to look up at the sky, to God, to humbly ask for help and answers but most of all for strength to endure it all.

With prayer seemed to always come tears.

And as the rain cascaded down, she wished it would wash all her worries away, especially the hate and the deep-rooted animosity for her mother that she had trapped inside of her. Once the downpours stopped, so did the tears. And somehow, not ruling out God, the rain brought her strength to move on past this moment. To fight and to endure the inevitable pain life would bring her way.

Also it gave her heart and the guts she needed to navigate through the world. Not to mention the courage to make the decision that on everything that she loved, from that moment on it was *fuck* Shelly and she'd take care of herself and her brother. By any means necessary, or God have mercy on her soul.

1

The situation would get worse—so much worse—before it got any better. So bad that at times Calliope wished that she was dead, but would quickly take it back, asking God to forgive her for her evil thoughts. The problem with that was if she was dead, who in the world would take care of Compton? Honestly, there was no one—no aunts, no uncles, no grandmothers, no grandfathers, neighbors, friends, teachers, or anyone who even cared. No one! The truth of the matter was that they were all each other had, and no matter what the circumstances were—bad, good, happy, or sad—there was no doubt about it, they had to stick together.

The morning after sleeping in the damp mildewed shed, the storm had passed over, and surprisingly Calliope and Compton were allowed back inside of the house. Shelly was in an uncharacteristically cheerful mood. It was so bizarre how she acted as if throwing her two children outside during a hurricane was no real biggie.

"Listen here, now!" she told her two children, with no kind

of sympathy. "Yesterday is gone and today is a new day. I don't want no kind of motherfucking grudges and most importantly I don't want no shit from you two motherfuckers." She leaned down and used her index finger to point at both of them. "You better not breathe one solitary word about where in the hell y'all two slept at last night. If anyone asks," she said, but Calliope wondered to herself, *Who in the hell would ask of our well-being? If our own dangone mother didn't care, who else would?*

The siblings just stood and gazed at their mother as she informed them of her concocted lie. "You are gonna say that you were at the babysitter's house. That's it. That's all. You got that?" Before either could nod or agree, "I wish either you two bastards would say anything else," she said as she stood over the stove carrying on with her immediate tasks of cooking eggs for breakfast, not even waiting for them to agree to her story. She was singing an old Chaka Khan song, "I Feel for You."

What made it even crazier was that the only thing worse than their mother's singing were her eggs and most everything else she attempted to cook.

At the end of the song, "Try me and see what happens. And you know firsthand I don't make promises." Before hitting the repeat button on the CD player, she said, with a smile, "Now, go on ahead and make yo-selves useful and set the table." Calliope thought that was strange because the last time they sat at the kitchen table and ate together was Thanksgiving, which was a good eight months ago.

Though Calliope did what she was told, wiping the table and getting the plates out of the cabinet while directing Compton to get the napkins and the silverware, she was still almost speechless. Calliope hadn't seen her mother in such a happy mood like this in God knows how long and couldn't help wonder where it all stemmed from. Then the source of Shelly's newfound Little Mary Sunshine attitude was soon unveiled.

"I have a surprise for you two heathens," she said, all smiles and bright eyes. She paused before speaking to them, with a Kool-Aid smile, which allowed Calliope's mind to run wild. Maybe the big announcement was she had gotten lucky and hit the lottery. Shelly played her numbers faithfully and maybe just one time, Lady Luck would show her face. If she did, they could move to a better neighborhood than the ran-down one they lived in, which meant better schools for her and Compton. If Shelly had indeed come into a windfall she could surely afford to hire a nanny to look after them, since Shelly never really wanted to deal with them anyway and never had any real interest in being a mother. Maybe she'd find one like Fran Drescher from *The Nanny,* who could help Calliope pick out clothes and take her to tennis lessons and those dance lessons that she'd always wanted. And if Shelly had an abundance of money, maybe she wouldn't be so mean and hard up for a man. Even for fourteen-year-old Calliope it was sickening watching Shelly run behind these good-for-nothing men who didn't want her noway. If she had money, she could fill her time with things other than chasing after her next meal ticket. Who knows? She may even take some cooking lessons. Heck, she could even hire a chef, and a live-in housekeeper, so that Calliope wouldn't have to be the maid anymore. She wondered if Shelly would buy them clothes and shoes so they could be fly just like Shelly was every day. Calliope was still thinking up ways that winning the lottery could make all of their lives better when Shelly blurted out with great pride and happiness: "Big Jack is moving in."

"Huh? What?" Too busy smiling for the cameras as they accepted the giant-sized check from the lottery presenter, Calliope wanted to act as if she had misheard her mother. Though Shelly didn't really care what Calliope's thoughts were, she wanted to make it clear what hers were.

"I said," she emphasized, "Big Jack will be staying with us."

In Calliope's mind, the guy that had been presenting the big check snatched it away at that very second.

"Why?" she shouted. It came out more like an involuntary spasm to her mother and the Indian-giving lottery cat.

Shelly ignored Calliope at first, wanting to get her point across. "Big Jack is moving in, and you two are going to act like you got some got-damn home training. You gonna keep this place spotless clean, so that if he wants to eat off the floor, he can. You hear me?"

Neither of the children spoke, and Shelly went on. "You are going to stay out of his way, and when you do cross his path, you are going to be kind, nice, respectful, and on your best mother-fucking behavior. You hear me?"

"Yeah, okay," Calliope said in a tone that conveyed to Shelly that it was certainly some bullshit, but she would oblige. And if she would, it was damn near written in stone that Compton would. After all, they really had no other choice. If they didn't, no telling what she might do.

"Don't raise your damn voice in my house," Shelly snapped at Calliope, but the bad thing about it was Calliope had not even raised her voice. "If you don't like the way I run things in this here house of mine, you can put them turned-over, ran-down Reeboks on and beat your feet." She got up in Calliope's face. "Don't your little ass ever forget who is the fucking boss around this bitch." Then she put her hand up as if she was going to smack her daughter. "You hear me, lil' girl?"

Calliope just looked at her mother and nodded. Then before they were finished eating the runny eggs, Shelly said, "Now, get the fuck up and clean this goddamn house before Big Jack gets here and starts to move his stuff in. And when he does, stay the hell out of his way." Then she added, "And don't beg for shit either."

Calliope hopped up immediately. She was glad to be excused from the table, even if it meant she had to go and slave. She hated Shelly's cooking with a passion and wanted no part of it. But her moving so quick was mistaken for her having an attitude, prompting Shelly to respond, as always on her power trip. "Lil' girl." She stood up too. "Don't you ever forget, as long as your ass is black and you live with me, that I, Shelly Conley"—she pointed to herself—"call all the shots under this roof."

To tell the truth and to shame the devil.

The truth of the matter was after Big Jack moved in, he called all the shots . . . every last one of them, even down to the kind of toilet paper they used. But the interesting thing was all the mouth and jibber jabber that power-driven Shelly had, she allowed him to. In a strange way, he turned their once dysfunctional home into a slightly less dysfunctional one but somehow making it an open-air drug market.

As soon as Calliope got home from school, she was allotted

one hour to make dinner. Other than that, the kitchen was pretty much off-limits to Shelly and the kids. It had been turned into a fully functioning crack-cocaine manufacturing lab. The powder cake was cooked with baking soda in pots of boiling water before being cooled off with ice. The kitchen table was used to package the products to be ready for sale. The final product was transacted with strange men of all races, sizes, and ages in the den all day, all night, seven days a week.

There was no small-time, nickel-and-dime money or drugs being moved in and out of the house. Big Jack, an already two-time felon, only sold big weight to major players around the city. In his eyes, if he went back to the penitentiary, they would bury him; regardless of the amount he was caught with, he would be up shit creek. So he had decided quite some time ago he was going out big or not at all. And his motto was to ball until he falls.

Over the next three months, Calliope and Compton were mostly confined to their bedroom, which was fine with Calliope, especially since Big Jack had bought them a thirty-two-inch television and had someone come and wire the illegal cable. This made Compton the happiest kid on the block because he could watch whatever he desired, all day if he wanted.

Big Jack always verbally expressed, "Y'all ain't my got-damn kids and I ain't y'all's daddy. Shit, I hate fucking kids." But he always bought them sneakers when he went to the mall and made sure the refrigerator was always running over with food and the cabinets with snacks. In the mornings, when they left to go to school, even though they had free lunch, he faithfully gave them lunch money.

In a twisted kind of way, having Big Jack there made Shelly treat them better, yet Calliope didn't look at Shelly any different. She still wasn't shit and wasn't a mother to them in any kind of way, no matter how much she tried to fake it. Nor did Calliope have the least bit amount of trust for Big Jack or the people who scored the drugs from him. The men would openly gawk at her, like snakes eyeing a delectable brown mouse. It made her so uncomfortable, and she knew it would be only a matter of time before one of them was presented with an opportunity and might try something forcefully. That was her biggest fear: that one of them would rape her and steal her virginity, which she valued so much. Though Shelly had never had a talk with her to tell her that she was worthy and how much she should value her body, somewhere, somehow along the way she managed to figure that out for herself.

One night in the wee hours of the morning, she woke up out of her sleep and left her and Compton's bedroom to go to the bathroom. She was wearing some short-pants pajamas and a short-sleeve pajama shirt. Nothing too revealing, but there was no way to hide her overdeveloped hips, butt, and breasts. One of Big Jack's workers, Joey, was coming out of the restroom as she was going in. He looked her up and down, licked his lips like she was a lollipop. "Damn, girl," he said.

Calliope ignored him, acting as if she didn't notice him or hear him. After she finished her business in the restroom, she opened the door to exit it. Before she could react, he had palmed her ass and then grabbed her and pulled her closer to him. He put her hand on his erect manhood. "Stop!" she screamed, trying to remove her hands, but he had her up against the wall. "Shut up. You know you want it."

"No I don't," she said loudly and firmly, hoping someone would hear her and make him stop.

Then he threw his tongue down her mouth, and that's when she tried with all her might to squeeze the blood circulation out of his penis. But his pants were so oversized that she couldn't do enough damage to stop him before he took his strong hands and grabbed ahold of hers. With his tongue down her throat, it was damn near impossible to scream. Instead she tried to kick the wall, to alert somebody in the house of what was going on, hoping and praying someone would hear and come and help her. For a split second he took his tongue out of her mouth, and at that point, she screamed at the top of her lungs, "Stop!" He ignored her and kept on moving forward. By this time he had his hands down her shorts and almost in her underwear, when Compton came and bit his leg. "Get off my sister." Joey pushed Compton's little puny behind down. With just that small distraction, somewhere the strength came. With all her might she kneed him in the nuts.

"Shit's too much work," he said to her, and looked her in the eyes. "You lucky it's the wrong time and wrong place."

"Punk ass." Calliope looked at him as he walked away. Compton came to his sister.

Then out of nowhere came Big Jack. "What the fuck you doing?" he said, wanting an explanation from Joey.

"Shit, nigga, she ain't nothing of yours, not yo daughter. You hate them kids."

"She in my house, under my fucking roof. And you don't disrespect me in my fucking house."

Before Calliope or Compton even knew it, Big Jack pulled out his black gun from behind his back and started to pistol-whip Joey. Big Jack caught a glimpse of both of the kids watching him. He stopped and pulled his gun on Joey, who had blood gushing out of his head and it looked like a tooth was missing.

"Get that bat from over there in the corner," he instructed Calliope, "and come here." She did as she was told. She went into the den, where Shelly was curled up on the couch watching television. She didn't budge, blink, or look away from her program as Calliope went to the corner by the lamp and got the bat. When she returned, she extended the Louisville Slugger to Big Jack.

He shook his head and rejected it. "Hell naw," he told her. "Now you beat him. Teach this motherfucker a lesson, so he knows better than to ever try some shit like that with *you* again. I want you to hit this sorry sack of shit so hard that he will not only think twice but he will warn other pussy-ass motherfuckers who see you in that light. He will warn them about even thinking of trying you."

Calliope had never been in a fight in her life. She wasn't sure she wanted to hit Joey. She was glad that she was out of his hold and just wanted him out of her sight. She hesitated. "Look, if you don't do it, I'm going to kill this motherfucker right here and it's going to be your fucking fault. It's up to you to teach motherfuckers a lesson. See, in this cold-ass world, you teach motherfuckers how to treat you. And this your first teaching gig," Big Jack said with much malice in his heart.

Calliope had no choice. She raised the bat and took her first swing and unleashed all the hurt, frustration, and pain in her on Joey, while Compton watched. She never heard the high-pitched scream that came after the first lick, but she did hear Big Jack's voice—"Shut the fuck up, child molester!"—which silenced Joey for the moment. But the next lick, she heard him plead, "Pleassse."

Big Jack interjected, "Don't beg now, motherfucker. You didn't hear her when she was begging, did you?"

Calliope had had enough, but Big Jack said to her, "One more time." And she did as she was told, then handed him the bat.

He took the bat and was silent for a minute, then called Compton. "Lil' nig . . . come here," he said, and when Compton got to Big Jack, he handed him the bat.

"Look, now." He leaned in and said in a tone above a whisper, "No disrespect, my lil' nig, but you know yo momma ain't shit for real, and yo sister all yo got. And it's up to you to let a motherfucker know he can't fuck with yo sister and do anything he want to her."

Compton wasn't afraid to strike, and unlike his sister, he didn't have any tears in his eyes.

"Teach that motherfucker a lesson," Big Jack said, still with his gun drawn.

To everyone's surprise, Compton started swinging and didn't want to stop. Big Jack had to intervene. "Man, you gonna kill him." And with a pat on the back and an approving nod, he added, "But that's right. You need to be ready to kill for your sister. That's all you really got in this world, my lil' nig."

Just like that, Big Jack took a couple of steps down the hallway and peeped into the den and called for his two workers to get Joey up and out of the house. He returned with the workers. "Well, lesson learned," he said to the kids. "And now get y'all's asses cleaned up and back to bed. Y'all gotta be up early in the morning." Then he yelled to Shelly, "Yo, make yoself useful, get some bleach and clean this shit up." It was apparent that she wanted to delegate it to the kids, but it was a direct order and she didn't have any choice.

"I want to kill him," Compton said, still on a rush.

"Killing won't make you a man," Calliope said to her little brother.

"I promise when I get big, I'm not going to let anybody ever hurt you." He knew that his sister was still a bit emotional, so he made a little joke. "This is why I'm going to eat my Wheaties."

"I know. But we just gotta always stick together now, and always watch each other's back. Thank you for getting that pervert off me. If you wouldn't came when you did, God knows what might have happened. "

She hugged him as they went back in their room and locked the door.

That episode wasn't the last of its kind, but it definitely prompted her to prepare for the next one. Big Jack may not always be around. It got so bad that for protection, Calliope borrowed three butcher knives from the kitchen. Although she tried to hold her pee until the morning, she always had a pocketknife with her when she went to the bathroom. If someone tried to hurt her or Compton, they'd not only regret it, she'd see to it that they lost a vital organ.

Every night after dinner, before going to sleep, they'd slide the dresser in front of the door. They didn't want anyone to slip into their room while they slept. They'd say their prayers and she'd promise her brother that everything was going to be okay. And she wanted to believe it, but living under those circumstances she knew it was survival of the fittest and she was determined to live even if it meant someone else would die.

2

One evening, Compton and Calliope were in the room watching reruns of *The Cosby Show* when Shelly came in the house with both hands filled with shopping bags.

"Honeyyyy, I'm home," she said, all excited and happy, caught up in this so-called fairy tale that she felt like she was living in. She had a good man making money, who people respected, who allowed her to have the finer things in life. This was the first time that she had someone who allowed her to be pampered like she should. Hair and nails done every week, and some kind of shopping every day.

"Yo, I'm here," Big Jack called back to her from his office, the kitchen.

Though Shelly always stressed to the kids to stay out of grown folks' business, that didn't stop Calliope or Compton from going to their bedroom door to ear hustle in on Shelly and Big Jack's conversation.

Though Compton would never want to admit it, though Big Jack was a bad man and seemed to be a shrewd, deranged person when it came to his business, there was something alluring about him. Big Jack seemed like a character from one of those hood gangsta movies, though he wasn't acting, he was the real deal. Compton always watched from afar the way Big Jack dealt with folks and handled certain situations.

Shelly went straight into the kitchen and gave Big Jack a long *Gone With the Wind* tongue kiss. "Hey, baby," she said, smiling. Then she proceeded to the Victoria's Secret shopping bag and pulled out this red sexy number. "Look what I got for you tonight." She gleamed. "I know how you like me in red and all." She smiled again.

Calliope and Compton turned their noses up thinking of their mother modeling the negligee. "Yuck," they both agreed.

Big Jack looked it over and nodded. "That's nice, real nice," he said, smacked her on her butt, and then asked, "And what else you got?"

Shelly was just as excited to share her shopping experience with her man, who had funded it all. She happily began pulling things out of the designer and boutique shopping bags, displaying all the things that she had purchased. Some of the things she modeled for him, parading everything around the living room. "Here, baby, these things are for you." She sat patiently as he opened up the bag and examined the things she had gotten him, waiting for his approval.

By the time she pulled the last thing out of the bag, he had a blank look on his face as if he was waiting for either more or the punch line. "What, baby?"

"How much you spend?" he blurted out, cutting straight to the chase.

Shelly's smile quickly went to a frown. "Umm." It was obvious she made it seem like she was trying to calculate the cost before speaking, but Big Jack knew better. See, he was a real G, in so many aspects of the word, and he had been around the block a few times. He knew that she was trying to run the pros and cons in her mind, as if she was trying to decide whether or not she was going to tell him the truth. So he nipped that in the bud.

"Look, baby. I ain't tripping on no got-damn money. Straight up! Never have. Never will. Believe that," he said, looking in her eyes. "Money don't mean shit to me. It comes and it goes. But the beauty of it is that I make money all day, every day. Hell, I makes that shit when I'm asleep."

The look of relief took over Shelly's face and out came a sigh. "I spent like six grand, I think."

"And this is everything you got?" he questioned. "No more bags in the car?"

"Yeah, and I did good! Caught some real sweetheart deals." Shelly was getting her confidence and excitement back up about her day of shopping. "Baby, this is over fifteen grand worth of shit. The malls had some killer sales," she said, boasting of the bargains she got. "And one thing about me, I do know how to bargain shop and get rock-bottom prices on certain things."

"I don't doubt it," he said, glaring down on her with a strong look of disbelief.

"What's wrong, baby?" she asked, putting her arms around him. She could see his dissatisfaction with her written all over his face, but she didn't have the foggiest idea as to why.

He didn't embrace her back. Instead he walked away and focused his attention on what he was doing.

"Baby," she cried out, "talk to me."

He didn't say anything. Just looked at her like she stank.

"Papi"—she went closer to him—"baabbbby," she said in a whiney voice. "Please talk to me."

He shook his head and she still looked dumbfounded. Then he spoke. "I'm trying to understand how the fuck you go to the mall and tear it down, spending money on top of money, and not as much as bring back either one of your kids a pair of fucking socks." He gave her a look of disgust. "Shit's ridiculous." He shook his head and added, "Real fucking ridiculous."

He might as well have stabbed her with a butcher knife or a spear because he cut into her. "Just fucking despicable." The emphasis he put on those words might as well have been some hollow-point bullets.

Now, if anybody else would have said that to her, she wouldn't have given two shits. But the fact that it came from Big Jack, the words tore through her heart. "You a poor excuse for somebody's momma. You some shit," he calmly and bluntly said to her.

Tears were in her eyes. The truth did hurt, and those words were sad but oh so true. She wasn't hurt the least from the actual truth about her mothering skills. Before she could respond, he said, "I knew you had your issues when I first met you, but I still fucked with you. Everybody got their flaws. I just . . . I ain't have no idea that you were that fucked up."

Wow! That really hurt her to the core of her heart. She was

embarrassed that he knew her secret and he called her out on it. She tried to kiss on him. "Baby, don't say that," she said, and tried to rub on his penis.

He grabbed her hand and forcefully removed it from his manhood. "Get the fuck off of me," he said coldly, and then shot her a look that said he meant it. "This the wrong time for you to be rubbing on my dick. Don't you know that shit results in making babies? And if you was the last bitch left on this planet, I wouldn't procreate with you under no circumstances."

Shelly stood there for a minute, looking at him, searching for the right words to say. But before she could find them, he stabbed her again with the words, "Get the fuck from around me." The words cut through her like a knife The tears began to swell up in her eyes and she did as she was told, but not before informing him, "I just want you to know that you really hurt my feelings." She tried to stand up for herself.

"Well, the truth . . . that shit hurt, don't it?" He questioned, with no remorse that he had hurt her with his accusations. "And furthermore, don't ask me what the fuck is wrong if you don't want the real got-damn answer. I ain't sugarcoating shit with you, man. The fact remains that you a selfish bitch with no motherly instinct or regard for your own damn children. That shit is a major flaw."

"You don't even like kids," she said.

"Yeah, that's 'bout right. But they didn't ask to be here either. And when you irresponsible, fucking with random clown-ass niggas raw dog, no protection, when you take that risk, the probability is that you can get kids from it. That's exactly why I make sure I keep plenty of Magnums around, 'cause I know I'm not trying to have no babies, with you or any other unworthy bitch."

Oh, that hurt. So badly she wanted to fire back. Not only did she know better, but also, after the way he had just gunned her down, she didn't really have any ammunition or firing power left in her. Before getting into a verbal war, which she was sure would lead to a physical one, she decided that she would make him regret those words, and she stormed out of the house. With one foot out the door, she yelled back in, "Glad I know how you feel, and you know what, we going to see what you be saying when you want some of this good pussy though." His first thought was to get up and go after her, drag her good-for-nothing ass back in the house and choke the life out of her. But instead he went to the door and shouted out, "Bitch, you gonna have to get on your knees and beg for this good dick, before I bless you with it." He grabbed his manhood when he noticed one of the neighbors looking.

She screamed back, from the end of the sidewalk, "You gonna miss me. You need me. And I bet you be calling me in only a matter of time." She was walking away from the house still talking smack. Shelly knew better, to do it from a distance and not in his face, because one thing about Big Jack, he didn't have a problem, none whatsoever, using his pimp hand to beat a woman, or a man for that matter, down for disrespecting him on any level.

He laughed, like that was the funniest joke he'd heard in a long time. "Yeah, I need you like I need a hole in my head."

He had enough of indulging in her shenanigans of the deadbeat mother. As soon as she slammed the door, he called out, "Callieeeeee." Big Jack never called her Calliope. He always messed up her name. She was sure that he couldn't spell it or pronounce it quite the right way, but to let him tell it, it sounded like a white girl's name. And it just made more sense to him that instead of constantly butchering her name he'd call her Cali, and not to mention it reminded him of California with her brother being named Compton.

She came out of the room. "Yes, sir," she said. He never really talked to her, and if he did it was only because he wanted her to bring something to him or go get something for him.

"Look, baby." He went in his pocket and peeled off six one hundred dollar bills. "In the morning, I want you to go and get you and yo brother some sneakers."

"I will," she said, taking the money out of his hand. "Thank you so much." She humbly smiled. She was sure that Big Jack thought it was for him, looking past Big Jack and at her brother who was peeking around the corner with a small steak knife in his hand. He was just as curious as to what Big Jack wanted with his sister and was using his own advice against him.

Big Jack shook his head. "I don't know why y'all's momma do y'alls like that dere. Shit don't make no sense at all."

Calliope agreed but didn't say anything, only tucked the cash in the back pocket of her jeans. She just stood there, wanting to take the money from his hand and retreat back to the bedroom. But she didn't want to be rude, so she listened to him vent. "Enough about y'alls no-good ass momma," he said, then went back in his pocket and peeled off a fifty-dollar bill. "Go on ahead and get on dat dere phone and order you and yo brother a pizza or some Chinese food or something."

Calliope didn't waste any time ordering the food. "Compton," she called out to her brother, "what you want on your pizza?" The two of them loved pizza, and it was a luxury for them to order it.

He leaned in and whispered to his sister, "Don't we have a lot of money?"

Big Jack heard. "Compton, man, order anything you want."

He smiled. "I want stuffed crust pizza. I want everything on it."

"But you not going to eat everything," Calliope warned her brother.

"Yes I is," Compton said.

"Okay, but watch, you going to get it and not want it. I'm telling you what I know."

Compton thought for a minute, because he knew his sister was usually right. "Okay, well, I want meat and cheese with pineapples and mushrooms."

Calliope raised her eyebrows. "No mushrooms, okay?" she advised Compton.

"Okay," he agreed. "I want breadsticks and chicken wings too."

She nodded, as she was on hold waiting to place the order.

"And I want soda." He pushed the envelope even more.

She smiled. Her brother was happy that they could get whatever they wanted. Once the pizza arrived, they sat at the kitchen table and ate every bite like it was the last supper. Compton was all smiles. It felt good that they were finally getting to live high off the hog. And they liked how it felt.

Once the two were done eating, they went back into their room and Big Jack went back to business as usual.

"Maybe Big Jack isn't so bad after all," Calliope said.

"But you said, trust no one." Compton looked at his sister with a raised eyebrow. Even at the ripe age of ten, he seemed to be wise beyond his years, and especially since Big Jack moved in, he seemed to have matured a couple of years in only three months.

"We still don't trust him or let our guard down, but at the same time, he looks out for us better than Momma."

"I know, and he cooks and makes sure we eat better than Momma ever did."

"You do have a point there, but that's all you really care about is your stomach anyway," she joked.

Compton smiled, knowing that he couldn't argue with that.

"Sister, I'm going to make a lot of money one day so we can always eat what we want to eat and so that you can buy whatever pretty dresses you want."

"Aw, you so sweet. I know we both going to take care of each other, that's all that matters."

"Yup." Compton nodded. "We going to have our own big money and when we do we ain't going to buy Momma nothing."

Calliope smiled and agreed.

"Maybe we will help Big Jack 'cause he do look out for us," Compton said. "We can repay the favor."

"He probably won't be around that long. He probably gonna

pack up and leave Momma," Calliope said, thinking of the consequences of the tantrum that Shelly had thrown on Big Jack. "If he do cut her off"—Calliope shook her head—"she gonna be worse than what she was before he came."

"I hope he don't, but he doing his business here, so he not going to close that down, he make too much money," Compton said, thinking about the money that he witnessed pass from hand to hand.

"You are so right, little brother. I hope so anyway," she said, commending her brother on such a smart call. Then there was an awkward silence between the two of them and she spoke again. "I was so happy when he took up for us, though."

"I was happier than a fat kid with cake when he made Momma cry," Compton said.

Without hesitation, Calliope said, "Me too!" and started to laugh, which prompted her brother to roll into laughter. They gave each other five and then began making their own entertainment. The two started their own theatrics, mocking their mother as Big Jack made her cry. Compton was Big Jack and Calliope was Shelly. The two were rolling in laughter, and they hadn't had a good laugh like this one in a long time. The two were so loud that Big Jack came to the room door. He tried to turn the knob, but it was locked. He hated when that happened. "Why the hell y'all always locking the doors around here? Y'all in there doing something y'all ain't got no business . . ." Before he could continue, Compton unlocked and opened up the door. Once the door came cracked, the laughter ceased. "What the hell is so funny in here?"

Trying their absolute hardest to stand up straight and still like statues, the two could barely keep their composure. "Nothing," they said in unison.

He searched their faces. "Come on now, share the joke. Between trying to keep food on the table and dealing with y'all crazy-ass momma, I could use a got-damn laugh."

As soon as Big Jack made mention of Shelly, the two lost their cool and started laughing. Big Jack shook his head. "A'ight now, y'all don't wanna share but I'm glad y'all laughing, for real though," he said as he walked back out the room. "And stop locking the doors and shit. I don't know if you think somebody going to do something to y'all or something. But on everything I love, ain't nobody going to fuck with y'all."

They heard him and appreciated it, but those words from him went in one ear and out the other. They knew they still needed to look after each other over all things.

After the kids finally stopped their jokes, they decided to settle down and watch some television. "You hear that?" Compton said.

"What?" she asked her brother, knowing that sometimes he was paranoid but he had great intuition.

"Like somebody outside our window." That was the thing about Compton, he observed everything. He used to be timid from all the screaming and threatening that Shelly had done over the years, but it had become paranoia. Calliope didn't take any of it lightly because she knew exactly how aware of his surroundings he was.

She peeked outside the window but couldn't see anything. "Boy, you paranoid. The boogeyman ain't going to come and mess with us. And if he do, we will double bank him," she sarcastically said to him.

"No, I hear it again." Compton was as serious as he could be.

She paused for a second, grabbed the remote, turned down the television, but didn't hear anything but the muffled music that Big Jack was playing while he was working the stove, cooking cocaine as usual.

The minute Calliope got back comfortable and was ready to tune in to her show, all hell broke loose.

Bam! A loud noise came from the front room, scaring the daylights out of both Calliope and Compton. Something or someone had penetrated the front door. Then came another loud sound. *Bammmmm!* By now Calliope had grabbed Compton to pull him close to her so hard she almost pulled his arm off. She didn't know what the hell was going on, but whatever it was, it wasn't nice. They took cover in the closet.

Meanwhile in the front part of the house, Big Jack, an OG who had been in the dope game for a real long time and was a vet to the streets, knew exactly what time it was. He was more than positive it was the stick-up boys and they were coming for him. But Big Jack, who was as fearless as they come, wasn't tripping at all because he knew just how to handle that. Anybody who knew Big Jack should've known one thing about him: that he was prepared at all times for any kind of ambush and wouldn't be caught slipping. Big Jack always kept a fully loaded Super 90 semi-automatic shotgun by the kitchen door in preparation for such occasions as these. He completely understood the nature of the game and the mentality of the non-money-getting dudes: if you're unable to *make* it, *take* it . . . or *die trying*.

And make no mistake about it; he was willing to do just that. "Motherfuckers, I'm not new to the game. I'm true to this, you motherfuckers!" he screamed, taking position fully ready for combat.

Before the wooden door was completely ajar with plenty of heart and gusto, Big Jack had charged into the living room, banging the shotgun at the unforeseen targets.

Boom! Boom! Boom! He blasted whoever he felt was coming for him.

"Mafuckas, you wanna rob me?" Then he shelled out another. *Boom! Boom! Boom!* The sound was so loud that the shattering of the glass tables and picture frames was camouflaged.

It was a true adrenaline rush for Big Jack. After each shot, another double R buckshot was slammed into the firing chamber. He went all out to protect what was his. Whoever was on the other side was getting a first-class ticket to hell.

This went on for about a minute and a half. Then the tables turned. Hell would always make its own reservations. As he went to take cover behind the sofa, bullets buzzed back at Big Jack like a swarm of killer bees, riddling his body in a matter of seconds, dropping him to the ground, making him almost beyond recognition.

Compton's eyes were the size of pancakes when the deadly fireworks erupted. "Maybe we should try to get out of the window."

Confused, but trying to remain calm as best she could, Calliope clutched the biggest of the three blades she'd hoarded. All she kept saying in her head was the Twenty-third Psalm.

An agonizing scream pierced the walls of the bedroom as if they were paper-thin. Then all of the sudden, it stopped. Calliope knew that the wail had belonged to Big Jack. She also knew that things hadn't ended well for him. Big Jack was dead. And if it was his time to go, nobody could control that. Wherever his fate took him, maybe he deserved it for the roles he'd played in all the lives he'd destroyed with the poison he sold. Whatever he did was illegal and worse to people who didn't pay him. She wasn't condoning it, but at least he allowed her and Compton to stay in a dry house and they got to eat whenever they wanted, and that was more than their good-for-nothing mother did for them. At the end of the day, in a weird way, he did look out for them.

But Calliope didn't have an extra moment to dwell on Big Jack's demise, or on her mother, for that matter. Her only concern was that she had to keep her and Compton alive and safe, somehow, some way.

Calliope prayed. "God, please help us." She put her back to the wall next to the closet door, gripping the knife so hard in her fist that she thought it might snap.

She prayed. Maybe they would take the drugs and money and leave them alone. Then she thought again: they were witnesses to all this mayhem. But not really, because they hadn't actually seen anything or anyone's faces. What incentive did these people have to leave them alive? Maybe they would feel some kind of pity that Compton and she were only kids. Her mind ran wild wondering, and begging God for answers on what she should do next.

Then, with her heart pounding so hard that she thought it was trying to jump out of her chest, she was never happier or more relieved to hear the word, "Police!"

Thank God, she thought. He was always right on time.

"Cease fire," she heard a voice say.

"Get on the floor! Everybody on the floor!" she heard them repeat a couple of times, and then footsteps were coming down the hall.

Once the door was ajar, she made their presence known.

"Don't shoot!" she cried out. "We're in the bedroom. Don't shoot us. It's only me and my lil' brother."

She wanted to shout, "Thank you, Jesus, God, Jehovah, or Allah." They were all watching out for them. They weren't going to die . . . and then suddenly it occurred to her, what if it really wasn't the police? *Oh, shit!*

3

Hold your fire! I repeat, hold your fire." Brad "Rusty" Cage gave the order through his two-way walkie-talkie. He was the lead officer of the TNT squad and was the last member of his team to breach the premises. One glance at the dead man sprawled out on the floor in a pool of his own blood was enough for Rusty to ID him.

He kneeled down and looked up with a wide smile of victory. "Yup, that's him." The corpse belonged to the man they came there to arrest. "Good Ole Johnathan 'Big Jack' Till." He shook his head. "A coldhearted piece of shit, who had been selling to a lot of key players throughout the city." He felt that this was definitely a milestone in his career and knew for sure that his superiors would be pleased at the efforts of his team under his supervision. They had wanted to catch Big Jack for a long time for drug trafficking, distribution, and murder. Although he had some other little petty charges, for the life of them, they could never really catch him with his pants down.

As Rusty stood over the body, he shook his head. "I always

knew this cocksucker would go out in a blaze of got-damn glory." He had respect for the bullet-ridden corpse lying there.

The rest of his eight-man team continued to search the house room by room while he gloated about what he felt was a major accomplishment, a dead dope dealer's body. "Well, fellas, I guess this was one way to get this motherfucker off the streets."

TNT was an elite tactical squad put together by the government to aid in the "war on drugs." Some people considered the squad's efforts an invaluable asset to the city and its communities.

Others called it a waste of the taxpayers' hard-earned money. The people could never understand why the governor would rather have billions spent on arresting small-time drug dealers and users, who usually got a smack and were back on the streets in no time doing the same thing, than on better uses, like schools, community centers, programs, and drug rehabilitation centers.

They claim it is a way to use the smaller fish to get the bigger fish but it's only politics because the news doesn't show the cartel getting arrested.

The search of the house went quickly, but methodically. "All clear," came a call from the master bedroom over the radio. Bathroom: "Clear." Den: "Clear." Kitchen: "Clear."

The entire house was covered by the special team in a matter of seconds, leaving the room where they'd heard the "call for help" for last.

It was protocol to be sure there were no hidden surprises—like perps with automatic weapons—before engaging with supposed nonhostiles.

Trained to go and ready for whatever was about to go down,

good or bad, sixteen trained eyes were focused on the remaining unsearched room, guns at the ready position in case the voice, who had tried to identify herself as a young girl, was being deceptive. Just last month a member of their team was ambushed by what was supposed to be an innocent, the sister of the suspect's wife. Mistaking her for a victim or a bystander, he ended up with two hollow-points to the chest for letting his guard down, a lesson they all learned from firsthand and would never forget. So, for sure every precaution would be taken in this situation.

Rusty issued the command to Calliope and her brother, "Come out slowly, and put your hands where we can see them."

After a brief moment—the door to the bedroom creaked open.

Calliope had never been so nervous in her entire life. She held her brother's small, trembling hand and stepped out of the room that had virtually been their prison for the past three months.

"My name is Captain Cage," the team leader said in a practiced, calming voice, "but my friends call me Rusty. Good Ole Rusty, and we're going to be friends." He tried to come off as nice as he could. Then he asked, "Is there anyone else in the room?"

Shaking her head, Calliope said, "No." But guns still rushed their bedroom anyway. One of them shouted: "All clear in here, Captain!"

For the first time since entering the house, the TNT squad relaxed, somewhat.

To Calliope, the air in the room smelled similar to the way it did after the big fireworks display at the Fourth of July festival she attended last year. She turned up her nose because the smell was getting in her throat. She told Compton to put his shirt over his nose, to try to camouflage the smell, and she did the same thing.

The police that called himself Rusty asked her name.

"C-Calliope," she said, wishing so bad that something could ease her nervousness. "This is my brother, Compton." She gestured to her brother with one hand while holding her shirt with the other.

When Rusty extended his hand toward Compton, the two were in total shock. Compton's hand disappeared into Rusty's. "Nice to meet you, Compton.

"Gunpowder, that's what that smell is. It's an awful smell, and we are going to get you out of here," he said, acting as if he was trying to be helpful, but she didn't trust him. Something about his shifty eyes made her nervous.

One of the members of the task squad radioed for a coroner. He recited the address into the headset, then tried to cover Big Jack's frozen body with a blanket before she or Compton noticed, but he was about two minutes too late.

The sight of Big Jack's body covered in a pool of blood would be a picture that she would never forget. Big Jack didn't look as mean, dead, or even as stressed as he'd been alive, Calliope thought. For some reason he looked like he was at peace. She wondered if she was crazy to think that he was okay with being dead. *I guess you had to be; you didn't really have a choice. At least his last few minutes of living, he did some good*

things and maybe God will overlook all of the bad things he did.
Then she thought again: *God blesses fools and babies, so Big Jack
might be okay.* Big Jack would like to think he wasn't no fool,
but in Calliope's eyes he was a fool for the way he went out,
gunning at the cops.

Rusty asked, "Where's your mother at?" in an attempt to
divert her attention back to him.

Calliope was in a trance, watching Big Jack's cooling blood
slick away from his lifeless corpse.

"Shouldn't the blood have stopped since he's dead?" she
asked.

"Your mother . . . ," Rusty said again when Calliope hadn't
responded to his initial question. "Do you know?" Calliope
didn't respond. "Do you know where she is?"

She was still studying the horrific scene.

Pulling her eyes away from the blanket that covered the
man who'd acted as their house warden but their protector and
provider as well, Calliope thought about Rusty's question for
a beat.

"Probably shopping I guess," she said. "Not really sure."
Shelly didn't share her daily itinerary with them. Oftentimes
they went days without even seeing her or speaking to her even
when they were in the same house, but Calliope didn't bother
to share that part with Rusty.

"What about any other family?" Rusty inquired. "A grand-
mother? Aunt? Cousin? Uncle?"

Calliope shook her head. "We have no one," she said non-
chalantly.

Their mother, Shelly, was originally from New Orleans. If

they had any family other than her, neither child knew of their existence.

"It's just us," Calliope said to Rusty.

At age thirty-two, Rusty was known to his colleagues as The Machine. Not because of the tireless work ethic he gave to the job, but more for his emptiness when it came to showing emotion.

"This is what's going to happen," said Rusty matter-of-factly, with the intent of trying to get the kids to open up to him. "There's no need to hold out on additional family because you think they are going to get in trouble or you are going to be able to stay with your mother. Not happening, at all." He shook his head and his pointer finger. "Unh-uh, no! Because even when your mother returns, she'll be arrested and booked for conspiracy to distribute cocaine, countless gun charges, and two counts of reckless endangerment of a child." He walked back and forth, and then slid his palm over the crew cut that used to be a mane of curly blond hair. He put his police-issued black baseball-style cap back on. "Being that you have no other family, we're going to have to have someone take you to Social Services."

Those words, "social services," tore through Calliope like bullets, but she tried to show no emotion. "Then what?"

"If a temporary guardian doesn't come, then it's farewell to this life you once knew, with family and friends. You'll be put in a home until you're eighteen."

The thought of being separated from her brother caused her stomach to pancake. *This can't be happening,* she thought. But the dour expression on Rusty's face convinced her that it was and there was nothing either of them could do to change it.

Compton, aware of the implications, squeezed Calliope's hand for dear life.

"You said you were our friend. A friend wouldn't do that. You a liar. Big Jack always said don't trust no police, ever. I don't trust you," Compton said.

Though those were her sentiments exactly, Calliope squeezed her brother's hand tight, wanting him to shut the heck up, because she wanted to try to appeal to Rusty to get him to work something out. But she knew that the ego-driven high-strung cop didn't give a damn, and helping two black kids out was the last thing on his mind.

For a split second she thought about just grabbing her brother's hand and running, but the place was surrounded and there would be no getaway, so basically at this moment, they were pretty much fucked and there was nothing that she could do about it.

4

The morning heat wave made the old-school mercurial thermometer look as though it were blushing, the temperature already stretching well into the nineties. Moisture in the air made it difficult to capture a restorative breath, so oppressive it almost felt as if one were trying to breathe from the bottom of a hot tub.

Just an average day in the heart of one of the most beautiful cities on the East Coast—but beauty was in the eyes of the beholder.

From Calliope's eyes, as the uniformed officer led Compton and her up a set of concrete steps that were hot enough to fry eggs to their grim fate, things couldn't have been more horrific. Yet, even in the grips of this tropical furnace, from Calliope's perspective, the world was coldhearted and frigid.

Once they reached the apex of the concrete hot plate, the officer held a steel door open for them. Then they went through a heavy smoked-glass door, with words on it that read SOCIAL SERVICES. Inside was as cold as the people Calliope suspected worked at a place like this—a place that began the process of shuffling disenfranchised children around like playing cards, inanimate objects. As far as she was concerned, the Social Services department was nothing but a glorified agent for the foster homes, where kids were warehoused for money with, nine times out of ten, folks who could really give a damn about the children's well-being. She had heard ten times more bad stories about foster kids than she had heard good ones—and most all of them had one common denominator: it was all about the money.

"Have a seat." The officer pointed them to the plastic chairs that were lined up against a toxic-green wall.

"What's going to happen now?" Compton asked his sister once the officer had hustled off to find someone to take the kids off his hands.

Calliope hadn't the foggiest idea of what would happen next. Well, she had a few ideas from the things she had seen in the movies and TV shows. And what one of her friends at school had told her about being a ward of the state . . . none of it was good.

She hugged her brother, absorbing his warmth, realizing that this may be one of the last hugs she'd be able to give him. She'd never lied to him before and she didn't want to start now. "I don't know what's going to happen," she said, "but I do know if I can help, hook or crook, that I won't let anyone split us apart." And she meant it that she would do everything in her power to make sure she hadn't lied now. Though she didn't have a juice card, an ally, or any power there. She knew that she wasn't a bad person and God was on her side and all the unnecessary stuff that she'd been through in her sixteen hard years of her life, maybe he'd have some mercy on them now.

And "everything in her power" meant anything.

"What if they try to—" She knew what her brother was about to say, but she cut him off before he could even finish.

"Well, you know what Oprah said, that you shouldn't put stuff in the universe that you don't want to happen, because you might bring it to existence. So don't even think it, Compton, okay? And I won't either, because if you think it, then it could come to life."

Although that's what she told Compton, as much as she tried, she couldn't erase those negative thoughts from her mind. And it didn't help that minutes went by at the pace of an arthritic snail with bunions. After what felt like a lifetime, but was actually more like two hours, they were finally seen. Apparently the folks at Social Services weren't all that social, and the services was tricked the hell up. She and Compton were in for two different ones. The only destination was that the known source of ass cramps were in front of a faux wooden desk. Behind the desk sat an antique white woman sporting a half smile that was not only as fake as the imitation wood but twice as stiff.

"Hello." The lady's pearly whites were funny-looking. Probably weren't real. "My name is Mrs. Daisy," she said. "From what I've been told, the two of you have found yourselves in somewhat of a pickle."

Compton turned to his big sister, face twisted into a mask of flummox, wondering what the old woman was talking about.

Even he knew it was impossible to be inside a pickle. "I'll explain it to you later, but it's just a matter of speech," Calliope whispered to her little brother.

"I've made a few calls," Mrs. Daisy continued. "Along with quite a bit of digging on my computer, old records and everything else, trying to get ahold on this situation for you two children. And"—she took an exaggerated look at her computer monitor—"it doesn't seem to be too many people we can contact concerning the two of you."

Tell me something I don't know, Calliope thought. *Hell, if we had real family, we wouldn't be here, lady.*

"In the State of Florida anyway. And the few we looked up in New Orleans weren't too interested in your predicament."

The Grim Reaper couldn't have been any more unsympathetic than this woman was.

A chill raced up Calliope's spine, a possible warning of the impending bad news.

Mrs. Daisy appeared to sense Calliope's expression and dredged up a spark of concern. "However"—she put her pointer finger up—"I was able to discover one local relative." Calliope, with raised eyebrows, quickly got attentive because she didn't know who in the hell that could've been, but at least it was one fighting chance they had of staying together.

Mrs. Daisy asked if they knew a woman named Mabel Moon. The name didn't ring a bell at all. "Well, she's your great-grandmother," the lady told them. "On your father's side. She's up in her years—but who isn't." Mrs. Daisy cracked her first authentic smile. "Ms. Moon has agreed to take temporary custody of you two kids."

They smiled and almost jumped out of their chairs so fast, they nearly knocked them over. God was good, for everything that she had ever did, it was finally coming back around. Karma was a wonderful thing, and Calliope was finally glad that someone in a high place was looking after them.

She didn't know a Mabel Moon from the man on the moon. But like the orb in the darkest patches of the sky, in their own path of darkness, Calliope was so grateful that she existed. Now maybe they could get the family structure and the family love they deserved. Who knows? Maybe this bad situation was soon going to be turned into a good one.

5

"This place sucks, sister." Compton's noodle-thin arms were crossed over his little birdcage of a chest. "The food. The people. The beds. The smell. The rules. Everything . . ."

Calliope raked her fingers through her brother's thick sandy brown hair, just as she'd always done when he was upset about something she couldn't fix right then and there.

And this was one of those times.

After no one showed up at the Department of Social Services to pick them up—including Great-Grandma Mabel Moon—the machination of bureaucracy kicked in. Mrs. Daisy said she had no choice but to advocate that the siblings be sent to The Home. This was the only place where the two could stay together.

The Home was the official name of the place, but all the kids called it Cemetery Grayshell, a dreary place where unwanted children were sent until they turned eighteen, unless they died first.

Prepuberty prison is what it should've been tagged, a training school for the real prisons that awaited most of them. This place was almost a prerequisite.

"I know it's bad," said Calliope, trying not to show her emotion at all.

They'd just finished breakfast: oatmeal that was as hard as cement next to a small slot of runny eggs. Just when she was positive that no one's eggs were worse than Shelly's, The Home had her beat out. "We're going to get through this, though, I promise." Those were all the words that she could say to Compton, because if this didn't kill them, they were destined for greatness.

They were out in the rec yard, a small piece of dirt not bigger than a small backyard in the heart of a major metropolitan city. They called it the backyard. Actually, the rec—a raggedy swing set with half of the swings missing, a sliding board, a basketball hoop, along with a few wooden benches—resided on about an acre and a half of flat red clay. But with nearly a thousand kids roaming around it felt a lot smaller and there was so much room for trouble with the idle time and no real supervised activities.

"Are you sure?" Compton questioned. They'd been at Grayshell for ten days, and Compton had already gotten into two scrapes with kids his age. Because he'd handled his business was probably why it had only been a couple.

Calliope wasn't sure of anything right now. Things had gone to shit so fast she hadn't even processed it all yet. Before the police raided their house, sometimes at night, lying in bed, she wished like hell that she and Compton lived somewhere else—anyplace but with their mother. Now she regretted wasting a wish. But if she was gonna believe in junk like wishes, then she also had to believe that they came in threes.

She looked Compton in the eyes and said, "Sure I'm sure."

PR system: "Calliope and Compton Conley, come to the administration office ASAP."

A horde of curious, mean, and lonely eyes flitted toward them. Why were they being summoned? Their eyes seemed to ask.

Calliope wondered the same thing. Sometimes if a kid didn't do one of his chores, he was called. Then put on room restriction for a week. She and Compton weren't allowed to share the same room; Grayshell was segregated by gender, no exceptions for siblings. So if either of them were put on restriction, they wouldn't be able to see each other. Not good.

The pace to the head office was a slow one. The hallways were poorly lit with high ceilings. No walk in the park, but at least they were still together, for now.

ADMINISTRATION OFFICE was painted on the frosted glass half of the wooden door.

Better than a bull.

The secretary looked up from a book she'd been reading. She seemed upset that she was being disturbed. She said, "Mrs. Crabtree wants to see ya." Then nodded toward another door.

Mrs. Crabtree was head mistress of Grayshell, the warden.

Compton looked to Calliope, wanting to know what she had made of all of this; Calliope shrugged her shoulders in response to the question marks in his eyes. At this point his guess was as good as hers.

There was only one way to find out what was going on, she thought.

Inside, the large office was lined with credenzas with lots of framed pictures of children with what she took to be their foster parents. And on the walls hung framed letters from kids who were successful and made it out of the Valley. Warden Crabtree sat nestled behind a chrome desk. Healthy green plants—all kinds—were carefully arranged throughout the space. The walls were painted bright yellow. The contrast, compared to the rest of the place, was as stark as heaven and hell.

Like Malibu Barbie dressed in a designer white blouse, black pencil skirt, and a touch too much makeup, Crabtree pushed a tuft of blond hair behind her ear, wearing a red-lipsticked, painted-on smile. "We have good news for you two," she said in a jolly voice. When the siblings didn't ask what it was but instead just sat there and waited for her to drop it on them, that wasn't good enough for her. "I said, we have good news for you." Calliope had no idea how Crabtree managed to squeeze the words through those thin, tightly pressed lips of hers.

The proclaimed good news came in the form of a gray-haired old lady sitting in the corner like Raggedy Ann.

"This is your great-grandma, Mabel Moon," the headmistress ceremoniously announced. "She's come to pick you up."

Pin-drop silence filled the space awkwardly.

The sheer volume of Mabel's dress—turned up red, pink, and green flower print—bitch-smacked the quiet clean out the room. And when she opened her mouth to say, "Is these my grandson's chi'ren?" her words were just as loud as the outfit.

"Well," Mrs. Crabtree reclined back in her chair and said, "why don't you lovelies introduce yourselves."

After getting a silent "okay" from Calliope, Compton offered his name and a hello. He was going to extend his hand but then changed his mind quickly before he had extended it.

"And I'm Calliope."

Mabel just stared at them—her eyes were volleying from one to the other as if she were looking for a sign. Something that would confirm that they were hers.

A spark seemed to show. Then some of the coldness dissipated in Mabel's glare. "You got Boo-dey Boy's nose," she said. She put her hand up to her chin as if she was thinking. Then she looked closer and nodded. "Mouth too. I guess you . . ." She studied them as if they were an exam, then came to the conclusion. "I guess you belongs to my grandson. Can't be too careful." This time Mabel gazed at the headmistress with no shame in her thoughts. "Mamma's baby, Daddy's maybe, and all."

The headmistress nodded as if she understood.

They didn't have much to pack; all of their things had been left at home. Well, where they used to live anyway, since they would have a new home now.

Mabel drove a nice late-model gold-colored brown Mercedes with whitewall tires. They hadn't been inside the luxury car for more than five minutes before she laid down the law.

"Now, we gonna be clear about this. Y'all ain't ask for me, I ain't ask for y'all. And I done raised all the kids I 'tend to raise, ya heard me?"

There was complete silence in the car.

"I asked if ya heard me? Ain't talking to myself, girl?"

"Then why did you come get us?" Calliope challenged, not wanting to be disrespectful but wanting to know what Mabel's real ulterior motive was.

Mabel went ham. "Why I what?" she asked, but knew good and well that although Calliope didn't know her from a man in the moon, she better not have responded to that part of her question. "Look, Ms. Growny Pants, I can turn this damn car around and take both you asses back if that's your way of saying thank you. That what you want?"

Mabel waited for an answer to her threat. Or promise. Calliope wasn't sure which, but she promptly said, "No, ma'am."

"No ma'am, what?"

This isn't going to be easy, she thought. "No ma'am, we don't want to go back," Calliope said.

"We'd like to stay with you," Compton spoke up.

"To answer yo question," Mabel offered in return, "I came and got you because you's family. I done helped or outright raised four damn generations of family, and neighborhood kids. More chi'ren that I can count. That's why I moved to Florida, because I thought I was done. Then I go and get a call saying I got family that needs me. Less they gon' spend they days in a kiddie jail."

Mabel jumped onto 595 heading west. Calliope wondered how long she'd had this car. Mabel drove like a professional, weaving in and out of cars, like she was really in a rush, to go where Calliope had no idea. But all she was going to do was to sit back and enjoy the scenery.

"I thought about it," Mabel continued once she'd navigated into the proper lane. "Wanted to say I could give a fuck about some damn kids that I don't even know. But you's family. Though it took me a few days to get here, that's why I came. Hell, I almost ain't come."

Calliope wasn't completely buying the family thing, but whatever it was, she didn't care. Her and Compton had their freedom, and if it got too crazy, at least they had the option of running away.

"Now, look, I ain't responsible for you and I'm not taking care of y'all. Y'all's on your own," she stated.

"Huh?" That part threw Calliope off. "Aren't you going to get a check for keeping us?" she asked.

The cold eyes returned.

"Damn right," shouted Mabel. "I'm getting a check. That's right, me, Mabel Moon. And don't think you gon' get one copper penny of it either. I'll supply the basics, but anything other than that is dead. And Compton is your responsibility. I got the roof, that's it."

"What about the food? They giving you food stamps?"

"You don't get it, do you? They giving me food stamps . . . they are mine. Listen, I'm providing shelter and you will be able to go to the doctor if you need because I can't do anything with the Medicaid. So y'all can have that," Mabel added. "The nurturing is on you, ya heard me?"

Calliope, by this time, knew the drill. "Yeah," she said. "I heard you."

6

"Posh" ... and "high saditty" ... those were the words that Calliope used to describe the neighborhood when they first rolled up in the driveway of Mabel's house. "Moving on up," from the theme song from the television show *The Jeffersons,* is all that kept playing over and over in her head. It seemed like Great-Grandma Mabel was doing or had been doing big things in her day. The Mercedes she drove was as clean on the inside as it was on the outside. The house was a turquoise split-level piece of architectural eye candy—it was one of the nicest, if not the prettiest one, on the block. The well-manicured yard was as green as the golf course.

"I hope she don't think I'm going to be doing all that yard work trying to keep this grass green," Compton said under his breath to his sister. Calliope nudged him with her elbow, and then gave him the evil eye to be quiet.

When Mabel pulled into the driveway of 8666 Sussex Way Road, she told them that she preferred to be called G.G. or Two

Gs. The kids wanted to bust out laughing, but Mabel wasn't kidding about her sobriquet. Calliope quickly found out that she was as serious as cancer about most everything that came out of her mouth, regardless of how outlandish it sounded.

In Mabel's world, providing the necessities meant: shelter, lights, and hot water, and honestly she didn't want them to use too much of that. Food and clothing didn't make it anywhere onto Mabel's list. She had specific times that the kids could wash clothes and they had to take showers while it was light outside, so they didn't have to use the light in the bathroom. Between the hot water and the electricity, it ran up her bill. They were only allowed to watch television when Mabel was not home, and that was providing that the house was spic-and-span.

After the police removed the yellow tape and right before the city boarded the place up, Calliope snuck into her former home and got what she could. Thankfully, out of the goodness of her heart, Mabel did give Calliope bus fare in the exact amount of change to go to the old house and return. "Go get what you can, and do the best you can to salvage y'all stuff because, I already told you, I'm not going to be responsible for clothing." Calliope wanted to ask, how many times was Mabel going to tell them that?

Thank God that she was able to salvage a few of her and Compton's things and some of the clothes from their old house. Luckily Big Jack had some things with tags still on them that she was able to sell to the neighborhood boys for a few bucks. It was only by the grace of God that money was still there in the jeans that she had on the day before all of the gunplay started.

Boy, were the two of them grateful. There was a God, and he was shining on them.

Now, living with Mabel was a hell of a lot better than The Home, but make no mistake about it, it was still quite a sandwich short of a picnic. Believe that. To hold up her end of the bargain Calliope had to pretty much quit school. She had no idea that making enough money to feed and clothe Compton and herself ate up a lot of time and trying to juggle the two were almost impossible, and so that they could eat, school had to go or be put on the back burner for now. At least that's what she told herself anyway. Her hustle of choice or necessity depending on perspective was boosting . . . utilizing the five-finger discount.

Calliope had never really stolen anything before but proved to be pretty skilled at it, after losing her virginity to the supermarket. Her first: a few packs of lunchmeat from the local store. Then came toiletries, underclothes, and cosmetics. Once she got more experienced at reading the floor workers and concealing the merchandise, she upped her game. The malls were where the real money was at and the labels and designers were all that she ever really longed for. It was her first real sip of the good life and it was the well that she wished to drink from— and with her talent, her taste for it was an acquired one. Getting the highest fashion in her possession for her and her brother was not only an adrenaline rush but also definitely her drug. Once introduced to her new vice, it became less about survival and more about feeding her habit: love for the finer things in life.

Six months hands-on on-the-job training and Calliope was a budding pro perfecting her craft to get any and everything that she wanted or desired. She was now able to get in and out in no time. She had it down to a science, figuring out the best times to go, and after learning how to use her time wisely, she started back at the new school at the beginning of the school year. From day one, both she and Compton had a huge fan club. People couldn't wait to see what they would wear. Of course neither Calliope nor Compton uttered a word of how they were able to afford such expensive clothes. So people, their peers and teachers, automatically assumed that their family was somehow involved in drugs.

Funny how with the fan club and popularity came not only lots of friends but foes, and most were haters hand over foot. Honestly Calliope loved every second of it. It all motivated her and she understood that rocking the flyest and freshest stuff to school would bring the haters and the stragglers and she welcomed it all. Compton was most appreciative of how his sister had him laced, and he loved the attention.

Calliope was sure that G.G. had noticed, especially the new huge posh towels and eight-hundred-thread-count sheets that she had brought into the house. But G.G. didn't part her lips to ask any questions. And Calliope took a page from the army: don't ask, don't tell.

Calliope discovered that one of the trade tricks was to dress the part; she had to rock the flyest gear if she didn't want to stand out stealing it. But being dipped in designer labels did get her noticed outside of the stores.

That's how she cut into a chick named Mocha. Fresh recognized fresh . . . it always took one bona fide diva to recognize another. Mocha lived a few blocks down the street from Mabel's house. The lady dressed like she should have been in the pages of a fashion magazine every single day. Her walk was something to catch anybody's attention; her strut should've been on a runway, the way Mocha acted as if she owned wherever her footsteps went. Calliope loved how Mocha carried herself with a sense of seductiveness. Calliope would watch as she came and went and studied her mannerisms. From up the block, looking down it seemed like Mocha had two boyfriends, both who drove European engineering. She always looked like she stepped out of some fashion magazine when she left and more times than not she returned with a few high-end department store bags. The stores that Calliope had mastered were the same ones that Mocha frequented.

Mocha turned out to be her best customer. Actually, Mocha was her only paying customer. "What you got for a bitch like me?" Mocha asked eagerly from the edge of the sofa.

Calliope unveiled two Roberto Cavalli outfits and three dresses from Caché.

Mocha, twenty-four years old with a banging body and a cuter face, only wore top-shelf designers. And had a dude wrapped around her finger that would gift wrap the moon for her if he could.

Inside, Calliope smiled when she peeped the glow that shone in Mocha's hazel contact lenses.

"I didn't even know these were in the stores yet," she gushed, grabbing for the YSL pumps. "These mofos are smoking hot. And this wine color is gonna go fab with that dress you got me the other day. How much?"

Calliope secretly envied Mocha. The girl had everything she wanted. And what she didn't have, she got. If Mocha had any problems at all, money was not one of them. The items she was asking about originally had a retail price of over four grand. "Give two g's." Calliope bartered high.

Mocha didn't bat not one fake eyelash. "I'm talking 'bout for everything, bitch—how much for it all?"

That's what I'm talking about, Calliope thought. Two things Calliope did as well as she boosted: dance and count. Utilizing the latter skill she quickly ran the retail numbers of the hot goods off the top of her head, cut the total in half, and said, "Oh, for you, bitch, just give me eighteen hundred . . ."

"Done." Mocha plucked a Gucci wallet from her Gucci purse and practically threw eighteen Franklins at Calliope. Then, already looking ahead, she asked, "Have you seen the new-style Cavalli jeans?"

Calliope had a pair already for herself, too bad she and Mocha weren't the same size, or she would've let 'em go with the quickness. She said, "I know the ones . . ."

"Can you get 'em?"

Calliope rolled her eyes at what she hoped was a rhetorical question, then answered, "Does a fat bitch eat cake?" Before Mocha could answer, "I will have them by tomorrow for you."

Grinning, Mocha said, "Cool. That's why I fucks wit you . . . 'cause you be 'bout it, 'bout it."

7

It was only a four-block hop, skip, and jump from Mocha's pad to Mabel's.

The words to the Master P song "Bout It, Bout It" echoed inside of Calliope's head the entire way. Mocha giving her such an endorsement was a big deal for Calliope. Though she would never admit it, she really looked up to Mocha. It was something about the way she carried herself that she admired.

Not that she was a groupie or a follower. In fact, she was far from it. But Calliope had to admit, it felt hella good to be recognized as a heavyweight by other people that really had it going on.

'Bout it, 'bout it.

Easing the key that Mabel had given her into the bottom lock on the front door of the house, she let herself inside the cool-blowing AC, welcoming the chilly embrace. If she could, Calliope would've hugged it back—because it was hella hot outside, and anybody who didn't have air—God blessed their soul.

The house was empty. That was one of the few pluses about living with Mabel. That lady never let no grass grow under her foot so she was always gone, if not out with her friends, then on some trip somewhere with the other golden girls, which allowed Calliope and Compton to come and go as they pleased. The siblings felt like they had the independence of living on their own even though they lived in Mabel's house and were still confined to certain areas of the house.

Today, Mabel was probably at bingo, Calliope thought, and—glancing at her watch—Compton's bus wasn't due for another twenty minutes. Enough time to run a quick shower and change clothes. Though still not of age, she had many responsibilities, and while there was money to go get, she was going to get it to take care of her and her brother. She planned to catch the bus back out to Aventura Mall to poach those Jean-Claudes for Mocha and didn't want to be wearing the same fit she'd rocked earlier today. That would sure send a red flag.

A couple of clerks wouldn't have noticed a pregnant elephant taking a dump, but it was better to err on the side of caution.

She took nothing for granted—that was a rule that she had adapted. She understood how nothing was owed to her and it could all be taken away from her in the blink of an eye.

For some odd reason, under the pulsating spray of the double showerheads, Calliope thought about her mother. She wondered what bullshit her mother was caught up in now. And what would happen if they caught up with her? With Big Jack being dead and all would she be held responsible? Even though sometimes it seemed they made the laws up as they went along.

They would find something to convict her of, leaving the kids or conspiracy. However, if Shelly was guilty of anything, it would be her unquenchable thirst to be validated by a man.

Calliope prayed that those traits weren't genetically inheritable flaws lying dormant within her DNA. She wanted to be nothing like her mother; in fact she wanted to be everything her mother wasn't. A strong woman, who made her own money, controlled her own destiny, and depended on a man for nothing. She only wanted to be with a man because she wanted to, not because she needed him to be her puppet master to contribute to her survival.

Though she had not been with a man and had never experienced the real love of a man, she knew what she would accept and what she wouldn't. It was simple like that. In fact she had started making a list. But having a boyfriend now was one of the last things on her mind, for now she had other responsibilities to take care of. Besides making sure her brother was taken care of, she wanted to make sure that she looked her best and felt her best. After all how could she have an above-average guy if she was subpar? So being the best Calliope on the outside and inside was the goal.

Her thoughts were interrupted by her brother's scream.

"Calliopppee! Where are you?"

He never sounded this happy when they were with Shelly. Ever.

"Coming out the shower," she called back to him. "Go make yourself a turkey and cheese sandwich while I get dressed."

She heard his feet scurrying to the kitchen, and then his voice: "Gonna eat some chicken tenders instead. You want some?"

"Nope, but make sure you clean up your mess."

Done toweling off, wearing nothing but her birthday suit, Calliope got an eyeful of herself in the full-length mirror on the bathroom door. Turned to the side then forward again. Returning her gaze wasn't the reflection of a little girl anymore. Her breasts were already bigger than a lot of grown women's, and they pointed north and got the attention of the North Star. And when she wore light Jean-Claudes, her butt turned the heads of teenage boys as well as grown men.

Her mother's genes indeed . . . they weren't all bad.

After a light dusting of MAC cosmetics, she put on Roberto Cavalli Jean-Claudes, and a white fitted Cavalli button-up shirt with cleavage peeking out. She slid on her strappy wedge-heel sandals, showing off her freshly painted pedicure. She was all set. Divalicious.

Compton was watching a rerun of *The Cosby Show* when she came down the stairs.

"Where are you going?" he asked as if she was his pimp.

"Out." She kissed him on the head and he quickly wiped it away. "Please, clean up your mess. You know we don't wanna hear Mabel's mouth. And don't leave out the house, okay? And if Mabel gets home before me, not that she'd ask, tell her that I'll be back soon."

"Okay," said Compton, eyes back on the TV screen. "But when you get home Ima kick yo butt in Madden."

"You wish you could." She tossed a pillow at him. "I got the last lick and ran out the house."

Inside the mall, hordes of people bustled about at frantic paces trying to cash in on the best sales.

Calliope hopped on the escalator to the upper level. Weaving back and forth, trying to dodge through the mobs of rabid shoppers, she slowed down once she reached the store that carried the Jean-Claudes that Mocha had ordered. Inside was no different than all the other spots packed like sardines.

None of their things were even on sale, not even on the first of the month.

The first thing Calliope did was scan her surroundings. The clerk: the same one from earlier. *Shit, I thought this chick would be off.* Three other girls walked the floor offering help to the people that looked like they couldn't afford to shop there, making sure nothing got stuck to their fingers, or inside a boosting girdle.

No one paid Calliope any mind. The lick she was killing screamed money and good taste. Babelicious.

She strutted straight over to the product she wanted, no aimless wandering around—fake window shopping.

With three pairs of Cavallis along with the pair in her hand, tightly folded, and tucked into what was practically an empty purse, she walked around the store. She hid the buzzers she'd removed under some other clothing. A couple belts and a pair of shirts and she was done. That was a wrap.

Now it was time to exit stage left.

Head held high, she waltzed toward the exit, and that's when the buzzer went off. One of the salesladies said, "Can I see your bag?"

"Sure," said a brunette too pale to be a native Floridian. The brunette handed the saleswoman her shopping bag. Probably a mistake, the saleswoman said with an apologetic expression and tone of voice.

"I'm sure it is," the brunette said.

Calliope exhaled, feeling a bit relieved, but kept it moving like she hadn't the foggiest idea what was really going on, until she felt a hand on her shoulder. "Excuse me, miss."

8

Her stomach fell like a fat chick in a broken elevator. "I'm store special security," the man said, identifying himself. "I'm going to need for you to walk with me."

What the hell he thought was so special about him? She flattered herself and chalked it up that maybe the store did realize that she was hitting them in a large way on a regular basis and the regular security wasn't seasoned enough to deal with a pro like her, so they hired this clown. He was a real cocky tight ass, who acted as if he was somebody and she should be intimidated by him. The truth of the matter was that she was scared shitless, not of him but of the consequences.

Calliope said, "There must be some kind of mistake. The buzzer didn't go off."

There was something familiar about the security guy, but she couldn't put her finger on it to figure out exactly what it was.

"I know," he said, "but I'm still going to need you to come with me for a moment. Then, if there's a mistake, we can get it all straightened out." She wanted to try to break loose, but the hold he had on her was tight like vise grips.

"Oh, my!" one woman said. "I knew that little black girl couldn't afford to step foot in this store."

"Well, can you?" Calliope boldly asked, totally catching her off guard. She stared at the woman as she got closer, making her way past. "I bet yo credit card bill is about maxed out, living above your means, trying to keep up with the Joneses."

Honestly it was nothing personal, but somebody had to say it. Calliope was already pissed that she had been caught and now this woman had the nerve to voice her thoughts on the situation, and to do it loud enough so that she could hear it. In Calliope's mind, she deserved it and even though she wanted to wallow in her own tears, Calliope smiled when she realized she had made the woman turn red and hoped that her heart was pounding just as fast as hers. The woman dropped her head and that stopped the rest of the whispering of the store's patrons.

Calliope couldn't be embarrassed at the awkward sneak peeks from the other patrons as she was escorted to the back of the store. The only thing she could think of was how in the hell was she going to get herself out of this major jam? If she went to jail for grand larceny, then Compton would surely be sent back to The Home, and God knows that would kill her.

Once they reached the small room in the rear of the store, the "special ops" guy removed the items from Calliope's over-sized Gucci purse.

"Now what do we have here?" he asked, and just by the way

he smiled, it hit her like a Mack truck; she immediately knew why he seemed so familiar to her.

"You're the police that raided my mother's house."

Off-duty, Brad "Rusty" Cage, in plain clothes, was taken aback. He was doing a little security work over the holidays to earn a few extra dollars. At first he was confused, then recollection shone in his eyes. Somewhat.

He asked, "You have a younger sister or something?"

"Nope." She shook her head. "But I got a little brother." She teared up. "You sent us to Cemetery Grayshell."

"Where?"

She informed him. "The Home. And you destroyed my life," she said with pain, conviction, passion, and anger.

"I destroyed your life?" He was surprised and shocked to hear that. He'd been working the force a long time and came across criminals and none ever affected him in a way where he'd taken heed what they'd say. They all came with their bullshit excuses and stories.

When Calliope saw that he had a puzzled look on his face, she took cold advantage. "My life wasn't the best before I met you. My mother wasn't too much thinking of us. And, yes, my house was a drug enterprise. However, at least my brother and I ate every day, and we didn't have to go to school hungry and get teased all the time."

"And that's my fault? And what does this have to do with me ruining your life and most importantly stealing clothes?"

"I have to take care of my brother, and our great-grandmother." She put on a show for this one. "God bless her heart, but she's old and is on a fixed income. That lil' money the state give her, ain't nothing on a fixed income, not to mention she has to get her medications and then my brother"—she shook her head and started crying real hard—"he hasn't been right since. Lord have mercy." She took one of the tissues off the desk.

"What's wrong with your brother?" he asked.

"That boy hasn't been right since our mother put us out and made us sleep in the outhouse in the backyard during the hurricane. He's been traumatized. Nobody wants to take the time to understand the poor kid but me. I'm really all he got."

He was quiet trying to assess the situation and she knew it.

"I begged you not to take us to that place, and you didn't give a damn. So see your consequences, what you did?"

Rusty couldn't believe this young woman was the same girl. She was so well developed, savvy, and beautiful. She had matured so much since he had insisted on having them removed.

"If you arrest me I'm not going to be able to watch out for my brother. He'll end up back in The Home, and God only knows what will happen. "

"Grand larceny is a serious offense," he said, remembering that he had a job to do.

"I'll do anything not to go," she said, knowing that he looked like he could be bribed. She was saying anything to get him to have mercy on her.

A funny look came over his face.

"Maybe there is something. If I could find you an easier way to make more money, would you be interested?"

"I told you already. I'll do anything," she said, unaware of how much things were about to change.

"I may be able to help you out. . . ."

That was seven months ago. Two hundred thirteen days ago to be exact. The same day she got caught slipping at the mall was the day she retired, bringing her brief and boosting—although fun, fabulous, and designer-label-filled while it lasted—career to a screeching halt . . . but it was the lure into a greater hustle.

Funny how quickly things changed, Calliope thought as she carefully applied a liberal amount of MAC Cosmetics to her cheeks, lips, and eyes. She loved not only the way makeup made her feel but also how gorgeous she looked in it.

Fear galloped through her bloodstream. "I can't go to jail," Calliope said, matching the face standing before her with the one of the lead police that had kicked in her mother's door. That was a bittersweet memory to add to her collection of them.

There was no sympathy for Big Jack, it seemed, in Rusty's eyes. He deserved to die a horrible death—he was an evil dude—but the chain of events forced her to woman up.

"If something happen to me . . ." She started to cry. "There's no one to take care of my brother." She thought about what she told Rusty that day in that back room as she searched the hotel closet for the right dress. She chose a form-fitting black backless number. After stepping into her dress, she pulled the fabric over her emerald G-string and matching push-up bra by Victoria's Secret and smiled. "Yeah, some dresses are solely for knockout purposes."

A hyper-developed body made it easy to transform from sixteen-year-old jailbait to the appearance of a twenty-five-year-old seductress.

And the perverted routine that she participated in once a

month had gotten a lot easier to be a part of than it had been the first time.

She reflected on that experience over seven months ago. "I don't know about this." Calliope had cringed within herself.

Rusty was a long ways off from the upstanding officer he pretended to be. He was one decorated cop with a hell of a dark side. He was as crooked and sneaky as a coiled cobra.

With a venomous smile that many mistook for comforting, Rusty said, "Think of it as role-playing. That's all you have to do. Didn't you always want to be an actress, in movies?" He kept trying to give her a pep talk. "Be like your favorite actress in a sexy movie." He wore his uniform, badge, and gun . . . the whole shebang. But he sounded nothing like a police officer—he sounded more like one of the street swindlers that he was trained to lock up.

And nothing Rusty said made any of this any less crazy.

"So what part of the 'movie' do you play, Rusty?" Intentionally forgetting to address him as officer, shoot he was the furthest from one. She wondered how long it had been since he'd forgotten that he'd been sworn in to protect people.

There was that smile again—the one laced with poison.

"Producer," he said. "Showtime is in fifteen minutes." Then he slithered toward the door of the motel room he'd bought. Before he opened the door to leave, he turned back around, and said, "Just remember your scene, lines, and most importantly . . . your role." Then he left the room, for the moment leaving her alone to stew in her fears

Shit! What have I gotten myself into? she wondered. *I should*

have just taken my chances and went to jail, and tried my hand with the judge. Then she thought again, *No the hell I shouldn't. This is going to be okay. You gotta do what you do. It's just that simple.*

The knock at the door startled the bejeezus out of her, even though she was expecting . . . company felt like the wrong word to describe what was about to take place in the room.

She was a virgin, not only sexually but to this whole new way of living and means of employment.

The virtual elephant sitting on her chest made it impossible to breathe. She panicked. Asked God to get her through this. Then another knock at the door. This time harder. "Just a second, I'm coming."

Breathe, Calliope.

Silently pleading for the walls to stop caving in on her, she cracked the door.

"Pumpkin?"

That was the name Rusty said he wanted her to go by. She wanted to scream, "Get me outta here!" Then she felt like saying to the client, "Fuck no! My name ain't no damn Pumpkin, it's Calliope. Now go away, pervert." She said, "Come in," instead.

The pervert didn't look at all like what she expected a pervert to look like. He'd probably celebrated at least about forty-five birthdays. Italian—most likely his nationality, and the type of designer suit that neatly hung from a muscular six-foot body.

"Nice to meet you, Pumpkin." He seemed to like what he saw, marching around her in a full 360-degree turn. He licked his lips. "You are so beautiful." Yet he still sensed her uneasiness. "My name's Roberto." When he smiled, his teeth were ridiculously even, the whitest she'd ever seen in person.

Roberto's eyes, black as coal, roved up and down the red dress Rusty had picked out for her. Then she saw it. It was just a flash, but it was there in those black eyes of his. A perverted lust, it was the same look Joey gave her when he was coming out of the bathroom and she was going in. It made her sick to her stomach.

"Do you want me to take it off?" She said it in a tone just a little above a whisper, and batted her eyelashes, just like Rusty asked her to say it.

Roberto bit down on his bottom lip. "Why not," he said.

He was supposed to be a ridiculously rich real estate mogul from L.A. that liked to buy young pussy. It was his only vice and he had this euphoric look as if he was on a high as he took her hand and spinned her around.

It must've been a while since he'd seen someone as young as her because his eyes almost jumped out his head when her dress fell into a silk puddle on the floor.

God was she scared, especially when she saw his manhood bulging out of his pants.

Roberto reached out, trying to cop a feel of her cinnamon-freckled ta-tas. She pushed his hand away.

"The money. Fifteen hundred up front."

Calliope couldn't help but to steal a peek at the huge bulge in the front of his pants. She tried not to imagine how much it would hurt inside of her.

She'd hoped that Roberto would change his mind, but he

gladly and quickly reached for his wallet so fast that he would've agreed on any price.

"Will hundreds be okay? Because that's all I have, baby."

Rusty instructed her to act like she was her favorite actress performing a sexy scene; it was too late to turn back now. Lights.

Roberto stripped down, never letting his eyes leave Calliope's body, which stood in front of him. He placed his suit over the chair.

Camera.

Then came the boxers. He was huge, a white cream already oozing from the tip; he showed disappointment and lust in his eyes both at the same time. "Sorry, I just couldn't help myself. But I'm going to take care of you and then we will be back in business," and that's when he reached for her . . .

Action!

From that very second, it felt like the world moved in slow motion. It was the longest two seconds of her life, and then the door to the hotel was kicked in.

"Police!" Rusty barged in, slammed Roberto on his naked ass onto the floor beside his polka-dot boxer shorts.

"You are under arrest for soliciting a minor and statutory rape."

He slapped the handcuffs and Roberto's face turned a deeper shade of red than Calliope's dress, which she quickly put back on.

Even now thinking about the way Roberto begged to "work this out," made Calliope laugh.

To keep the scandal out of the papers Rusty taxed Roberto a mint: twenty Gs and Rusty played fair and broke her off five

Gs. It wasn't half, but it wasn't bad either. Every month after the first time seven months ago, Rusty somehow managed to rustle up another mark. Where he got them? She had no idea.

Glancing up at the clock made her realize that she had to get herself ready. She took her brand-new Manolo Blahnik stilettos out of the box and strapped those bad boys on and was out the door.

It was that time of the month. . . .

9

"Five hundred," Moo-Moo exclaimed, almost not believing his eyes when he caught sight of the fat grip his best friend was toting. "Where'd you get so much bread?" he asked in a lower voice, scanning their surroundings to make sure no one was clocking them.

Compton stuffed the money back into the pocket of his jeans.

The two had met over a year ago at school. Moo-Moo was Haitian and lived with his older brother, Jean-Claude. Both of his parents were deceased. The absence of that guidance cohabiting with grief was the glue that binded the two boys together. Other commonalities would unveil over time.

"Calliope hit me off. I'm s'posed to go get those new Jordans and some gear. Gotta stay fresh kid." That was his best corny, fake New York accent.

Moo-Moo smiled at the diss. Florida cats weren't too crazy about New Yorkers, which was crazy because there were so many people who had migrated from up north—why they all couldn't just get along? Too be honest, the only folks Floridians disliked more than cats from the Big Apple were Cali dudes, and the feeling was mutual among each state.

"Check dis out . . ." said Moo-Moo. Compton could see the gears in full tilt inside of Moo-Moo's noodle. "Me get a monster thought," Moo-Moo finished.

Moo-Moo was barely a year older than Compton. He was only thirteen, but wise to the streets way beyond his years. And as a result of their closeness, Compton's street IQ quickly rose.

Compton asked, "That is it?" Sensing that it was something big. That's the way Moo-Moo ticked if it was something big. That's the way Moo-Moo's mind ticked, go big or go home.

And more times than not, his ideas were something that could potentially get them into even bigger trouble.

But even Compton had to laugh when Moo-Moo said, "Farming."

"Dude you funny as hell." Compton couldn't stop cracking up, then he noticed that Moo-Moo was serious . . . as HIV in Miami.

"What, man? Go on ahead and spill the beans." Compton had to know. "What we gonna grow? And better yet, what we gon' do with it after we done growing it?"

Undaunted by Compton's skepticism, Moo-Moo didn't miss a beat.

"Cabbage," he said. "We take that seed money in you pocket, invest with me brother, and watch our cabbage grow bigger and bigger."

Now Compton understood why his boy was so stone-faced. "You want to buy work from your brother." It was more of a statement than a question. They had done a lot of crazy things but selling drugs hadn't been one of them.

Moo-Moo broke it down like this:

"You know me brother, Jean-Claude got the weight in coke. We give 'em the nickel you got een yo pocket and he looks out for us with a famlee discount."

Moo went on to explain that he was certain that he could convince his brother into giving them two ounces for the money. "Cooked up we can pull een three Gs easilee."

"If we don't get robbed or killed first," Compton added. "This's Pork and Bean Projects."

"Jean-Claude runs the city," Moo-Moo countered. "We got the protection of his name and goon squad off top. These cats not stupid." Compton was thinking of the advantages and the consequences when Moo-Moo said, "I tell yo what."

It didn't hurt to listen, he thought.

"We flip the bread one time," Moo-Moo continued. "If you not cool then, we stop. You are cool, we step up. Deal?"

"Let me think about it."

They slapped hands.

"No doubt," said Moo-Moo, both knowing their premiere into the sport of trapping was soon to begin.

10

Cell phone ringing...

Calliope plucked it up from the end table by the third chime. "Hello?"

"A change in the meeting spot," Rusty said through the jack. A beat of silence passed. Another pause of silence passed before Rusty could feel her apprehension, said, "Not to worry. It'll be at a public restaurant in South Beach."

Calliope asked, "Why do it different?" Her whole vibe changed up.

Up until now, the routine had always been the exact same way. The johns show up at the room. She gets him in a compromising position—which usually meant unclothed—then Rusty busted in, caught them with their pants down.

"Sometimes you have to call an audible," Rusty said. "Take him back to the room for a surprise dessert. It's as simple as that."

It shouldn't be much to it, Calliope reasoned. She was so over this and really wanted out. Nothing about it felt right, and she wished that this wasn't what she had to resort to, to take care of her brother. But the pay and the labor were damn sure better than flipping burgers at Burger King. She sighed, thinking how she had cramps and wanted to just stay home under the covers watching a movie, but she knew duty called, and nobody was going to make it happen for her and Compton but her. "Okay," she said, "give me the address to the restaurant."

The taxi ride to South Beach couldn't end quickly enough; the vent blew warm air and the Jamaican behind the wheel drove like he got his permit at the dollar store.

Thank God, she had to give praise to him, when the Jamaican reached the destination.

"Twelve dollars," said the driver in barely recognizable English.

Calliope got out of the heat box, handed him a twenty through the window. "Get the air fixed." She walked away not bothering to wait for the change.

To her, Asia de Cuba, with its Alice in Wonderland décor, seemed too gimmicky. The hostess asked if she was dining alone.

She answered, "No, I'm supposed to meet Mr. Travoski." Calliope had no idea what the man looked like. *Dang I should've thought to ask Rusty.*

The hostess beamed a canned smile. "Yes, ma'am. Right this way," she said. They stopped at a table for two near a back wall. The man seated there was easy to recognize, being the only Russian in the place.

The Russian stood up to greet her. "Aahhh, Pumpkin—so good of you to make it." He pulled out her chair. Calliope took a seat. "How rude of me," he said once back in his own chair. "My name is Mikile Travoski. Good to make your acquaintance." She was impressed with his bright smile along with almost perfect English.

Calliope returned the pleasantries. Glad that the air in the restaurant was pumping full blast, she could feel the light sheen of perspiration on her neck and back start to dry.

"Drinks?" Mikile held up a glass half-filled with a clear liquid over ice. "Again," he said, "my apologies. For not waiting until you joined me to imbibe."

"I don't imbibe, " Calliope said, mirroring Mikile's fancy word for drinking, and she knew better than to mention that legally she wasn't old enough to indulge anyway. "Not alcohol anyway. But I'll have a Coke . . . Coca-Cola that is." She specified because she knew these guys were used to women in these kinds of situations indulging in drugs, but she wasn't one of them.

He seemed to study her features with his dark dissecting eyes and dilated pupils. Calliope felt uncomfortable under his stare. Then his glare transformed. It went from hard as iron to cottony soft.

After studying the menu—with not nearly as much scrutiny as he'd used on her—Mikile said that she hoped she had found something because he was ready to order.

Mikile went with a Cantonese-style whole yellowtail snapper steamed in banana leaves with shitake mushrooms. Besides the banana, Calliope had never heard of any of it before. Aside from the once-a-month meeting with the johns, Rusty always took her out one time a month, independently of them working, to introduce her to the finer things, just to make sure she knew how to carry herself when she encountered these financially set men.

After conferring with the waitress for a minute or so, she said, "I'll try the clams and the rock shrimp."

"Excellent choice," said the waitress.

More people poured into the establishment; a family of four, three girlfriends, and a biracial couple were all seated at various tables.

Calliope was wondering if Rusty was watching when suddenly her phone vibrated, and as soon as it did, he said, "You better check to make sure everything is okay."

It was a text from Rusty: "Are you ok?"

"Everything's okay." She offered a slight smile.

Once the food came, Mikile could not resist the cuisine. He had his face so deep in his snapper that Mikile paid her little attention when she thumbed back a response to the inquiry, careful not to bring the phone above the table. "On the main course."

But he had peeped her working the keypad, "Who are you communicating with?" Only a half smile. "Boyfriend?" he questioned.

That threw her for a loop, then her mind started to run wild. What if he asks to see her phone? Trying to get his mind on other things, she tamed her thoughts. Calliope teased. Still not legal but so quick on her feet. "You're not the jealous type, are you?" she asked, pouting her lips.

"Do I have reason to be?" he said in a playful way. "Whatever it is trying to steal your attention away from me . . . it is too late. I'm here—with you—he's elsewhere, wishing he's where I am at this very minute."

Who knew Russian men could be so smooth? Calliope milked the moment, knowing he really wanted an answer to his initial probe.

"He," Calliope said, dragging the pronouns, "was a she."

"Oh?"

But it was a curious "Oh." *Like, I'm open to threesomes* type of "Oh."

"Now I'm the one that's jealous," she quickly pouted. "I'm not enough for you?"

The bashful smile was confirmation that she'd read him correctly.

"Pumpkin, my darling, you're enough for any man." He downed a swallow of vodka like it was water and it seemed to have no effect on him.

Like yesterday, dinner was a thing of the past.

"Are you ready for dessert?" she asked, her meaning as clear as crystal.

"I'm more than willing to pay for the extra time I've taken." He spoke softly so that no one overheard.

"I didn't mean it like that. Actually, it was good food, and even greater conversation. But since you brought it up, time *is* definitely money," she said coquettishly.

A good sport, Mikile had adopted.

"I can't argue with the truth," he said. "Your place or mine?" She hadn't thought about what she would do if he wanted to change where their supposed rendezvous would take place.

Mikile had a hired car waiting for him. As soon as they

walked out of the restaurant, the driver jumped out of the driver's seat to open the door for them.

When Calliope gave the driver the address, that's when things got complicated.

"So stupid of me," Mikile said, patting his pockets as if he'd misplaced something. "I left my billfold with my cash in it at the hotel I'm staying. No cash."

He'd paid for dinner with an American Express credit card so Calliope had no way of knowing if he was telling the truth about not having cash.

This wasn't part of the plan. What does she do?

"My hotel is right around the corner," Mikile said as if there were no problem. "We can play there. I'll pay you extra. And pay for your cab ride afterward."

Getting impatient, the driver said, "The meter's running. Where's it gonna be?"

Mikile looked at her with those probing eyes of his and lifted a brow.

Sometimes you have to call an audible.

The driver wasn't the only one getting impatient. "Well, Mikile," he pushed.

Under the pressure of the rush, Calliope opted for the audible.

"Okay." She agreed but reluctantly said, "Your place it is." She knew she'd just given up the home-field advantage, but what choice did she really have? There was nothing she could have said that wouldn't have shouted "red flag" to the man. She knew she just had to text Rusty as soon as she could when she got to his room and hand off the new play, so he could get into position.

No problem.

Like Mikile had said, he didn't have to go far. The driver gassed the Benz down a ramp that ended at the mouth of a sublevel parking area. Found a spot, beside a 6 series BMW, facing the wall. He killed the engine. "We're here. Told you it was close by."

An awkward silence filled the cabin of the Benz. It was weird, like a first date or something. They both felt the clumsy discomfort of what was about to happen next, then it passed.

They climbed out of the Mercedes. Dim lights made it difficult to make out the entire area. Painted on the cement columns were arrows, pointing out the direction of the elevators.

Calliope was beginning to second-guess herself. She didn't really have a reason because Mikile had been nothing but a gentleman, but still . . . she was putting herself in a vulnerable position no matter the way she looked at it.

What? she thought. *Stop being so paranoid. You've done this plenty of times. Girl, you got this.* The truth of the matter was that setting these desperate perverted men up was starting to get the best of her. Though she was not really a victim, and she felt sorry for the girls who had been taken advantage of by these kinds of men. And the girls who were being pimped and having to deal with these johns and their creepy desires against their wishes, so having Rusty come in there and shake them down, oh well, that's what the hell they get. But at the same time her luring men to the rooms was still not only wrong but deceptive and dangerous . . . and she knew that she needed to quit while she was ahead, because one day she may not be so lucky in such a vulnerable position.

On the elevator, Mikile pushed 3. Calliope felt a lot more at ease once the door opened and the bright sun washed away the baleful ambient of the close quarters. "My room is at the end of the walk," Mikile said, leading the way as she followed. Though she didn't show it, she was hoping and praying that Rusty was somewhere lurking and ready to get this over with.

As they ambled along, Calliope realized that entry to all the rooms were gained from the outside, similar to the motel that Rusty had usually arranged her to be in. But this place was much nicer and it was on the bay.

If Mikile had been staying in a traditional hotel where the rooms were inside, she didn't know what she'd do. She hadn't thought of that until now.

Suddenly, Mikile stopped in front of a turquoise door: room 326.

He asked, "You okay?"

"As cool as a fan," she lied right through her teeth.

He pulled out a card key. "Good," he said, sliding the magnetic card into the slot. "I only bite if you want me to."

When the light on the lock switched from red to green, Mikile opened the door. "After you, my lady."

"Why thank you, my lord."

The room was awkward. A king-sized bed was the first

thing Calliope saw. *How convenient,* she thought. But there was more than just a bed. The bedroom opened into a full-sized luxury condo with a spacious kitchen and living room with a double-sided fireplace with a view of the bay.

Mikile got comfortable, slipping off his suit jacket and pouring himself a drink of vodka and ice.

He offered her something to drink. "I got orange juice. No Coke," he said. "None that you can drink anyway." He laughed.

She hadn't noticed how muscular and buff Mikile was until that moment. His tailored suit shirt clung to a lean muscular body.

"Juice would be fine." She copped a seat on the sofa. Mikile turned the AC on high, then flipped the gas fireplace on for symmetry and ambience.

"One orange juice, coming up now."

She had her game face on. "Cool. You mind if I use the restroom?"

With his face in the refrigerator. "It's next to the bedroom."

The bathroom was equipped with a Jacuzzi and a glass-encased shower. It was like a water park, Calliope mused. Then she locked the door behind her and quickly plucked the phone from her purse. She texted Rusty the name of the place along with the room number.

As an afterthought she texted: "Don't trip . . . had to make an audible."

Her phone vibrated immediately.

"Be right there!"

For the first time since being inside of Mikile's suite, she exhaled. Waited a few more minutes, she flushed the toilet, washed her hands, gathered her composure, and unlocked the door.

Mikile was waiting for her. "I thought you'd fallen in," he said.

She casually said with a smile, flashing her pearly whites, "A girl has to freshen up, don't she? And where's my orange ju—"

It felt like a hammer slamming into her side. He rocked her so hard all the air evacuated her lungs like it was running from a burning building.

Crack!

Mikile punched her again, this one may have fractured a rib. She tried to scream for help; there wasn't enough air in her lungs to push the words out. On wobbly legs she fell to the floor. curling up into a human ball.

Why is he doing that to me? Instead of an answer, she got kicked hard. She was so caught off guard and could never pull it together to really fight back. All she could do at that moment was pray to God for help and for strength.

Mikile bent down and yanked the bottom of her dress up until it caught under her armpits.

God must've been busy, because it only got worse for her.

Next, he ripped her panties away and the sight of Calliope's copious, bare ass turned him on. His tongue hung out his mouth like a dog.

Her body a magnum opus in its own right—got his dick rock hard. He undid his zipper; Mikile liked his girls young.

He straddled her like she was a horse and he was about to give her the ride of her life.

God knows this wasn't the way she wanted to lose her virginity. This wasn't how she had pictured it at all. All those times she'd imagined how it would go down and this was what it was coming to. Karma had a funny and ironic sense of humor.

The strong smell of vodka jumped off his breath and pores, so close to Calliope's nose, acting like a smelling salt. Mikile was so busy admiring her body; he didn't notice her hand easing into her purse. She found what she'd been searching for.

This might be my only chance, she thought, and make no mistake about it she was going to give it all she had. She lit Mikile's ass up with fifty thousand volts from her personal taser.

He screamed like a little girl, his wail probably resembled one of the little jailbait girls he had violated in the past, when those volts got a hold of him and he jumped back off her before collapsing in a heap.

"Police! Don't move," she heard, just in the nick of time.

Rusty had finally made it in with his gun drawn. Better late than never.

Rusty quickly surveyed the surroundings, eyes flitting from Calliope's back to Mikile, back to Calliope.

"Fuck!" Rusty footed Mikile in the face with all his might, causing a tooth to fly out of his mouth and carom off the wall. He cuffed Mikile's hands behind his back and then kicked him again. Again and again, then all of a sudden the dynamics changed.

Phut!

To everyone's surprise, Mikile wasn't the only Russian in the room. He had a friend hiding in the closet, with a gun.

The silencer shot Rusty in the back of the head, the bullet exiting between his eyes. The dirty cop never knew what hit him.

The Russian, this one shorter and rounder, sauntered toward Calliope with the smoking Desert Eagle still in hand. Her very last thought was her brother. Then the Russian popped her.

11

Pork and Beans Projects—or Cocaine City to some—was an apartment assigned for the abundant accessibility of the moneymaking narcotic, which was readily available, hard or soft, wholesale or retail, weight or pieces, 24/7.

Pipers stood in an orderly line to score. Compton took the bread from their anxious mitts while Moo-Moo forked over the work, chopped and bagged in mini ziplock bags twenty feet away, by the end of one of the housing units. This was a method of hand-to-hand trapping that was most common on the street, primarily implemented to reduce the odds of either person from wearing a direct sale charge if they got pinched for selling to an informer.

Having a fat pocket full of wrinkled, sweaty, balled-up dough, Compton was beginning to think maybe this wasn't a bad idea after all. He and Moo-Moo had been posted up barely more than two hours and already had made their money back ten times over and were still batting a thousand.

Jean-Claude, Moo-Moo's brother, an already made man,

had given the boys a good price, his blessings, and protection. It was no secret that not too many people (in their right mind) wanted to be on Jean's bad side. The word had been put out loud and clear: fuck with Moo-Moo and Compton (his baby Gs), and one's days aboveground are at their end.

Everybody knew that Jean didn't bluster with idle threats, only promises.

Compton paused to answer the phone on his hip. "Yo?" The piper next in line bit down on his lip, annoyed that he had to wait. He wanted to cop, satisfy his jonesing, and go, make it back to the grocery store to lift some more steaks.

Five seconds dragged by before the voice on the other end of the cell said anything.

"Comp . . . t?"

Was all that was said, so low, the single word almost wasn't audible. But the voice on the other end of the phone was un-mistakable.

"Calliope?" he questioned. "What's up, sis?" She sounded like death.

ROOM 326

Calliope, in a state of delirium, managed to convey the name of the inn and the room number. "I need your help," was the rest of the message, then nothing. A panicked Compton shut down shop immediately and though he had no real details he hipped his friend to the life-or-death business at hand.

Moo-Moo said, "You ain't going to go anywhere without

me." He was clueless of exactly what they were running into, but knowing they needed to get there yesterday. Moo-Moo wasn't anybody's fool by a long shot and got his brother Jean on board.

The door to room 326 was slightly ajar when Jean, Moo-Moo, and Compton arrived. The hotel was damn near a ghost town, except for a doting couple in the pool below doing naughty things, not wanting to be seen themselves.

Inside the room was a far different atmosphere. Everything was quiet and the picture was still. Jean wasn't deceived by the stillness, he was getting prepared for whatever was waiting for them there, and he had already slipped his gat from his waist and cocked it.

Compton called out his sister's name, "Calliope!"

Just on the other side of the bedroom, with his top popped and stretched out, was a roller, in full uniform. He was beyond help. Then Compton laid eyes on his sister. She was just a few feet away from the police officer. Scared shitless, he ran over to her, not sure if she was dead or alive.

He gently cupped her head with his hand. "Wake up, Cal, please, I'm begging you," he said with tears welling up, in his eyes.

She was bleeding from the head, bruised up, and half-naked, a sight that no brother should ever have to see.

While Compton held his sister's battered body close to him, Jean methodically searched the rest of the suite. Whoever was there was gone now and had made away with a fast getaway. He made his way back to the two siblings. Though Compton always talked about his sister, Jean had never met Calliope before. Even in her severe condition Jean could tell that she was a looker. He felt for a pulse and it was faint.

"She's alive," Jean said with relief, and acted fast. He picked her up and said to Moo-Moo and Compton, "Wipe down everything you think you might have touched. We outta here."

Neither Jean, Compton, nor Moo-Moo knew what had taken place there but they all were in agreement on one thing: a room with a half-lifeless juvenile girl and a fully smoked pig isn't the place anyone—especially any of them—wanted to be found in.

12

The glass tower was the nicest residential area in Brickell. And apartment 4118—forty-eight floors up—had been designed by professional decorators with high-end swanky ultra-modern furniture, rugs, and paintings and was one of the nicest in the building.

Inside of one of the four bedrooms, resting on top of a Thomasville queen-sized bed, Calliope coached her eyes open. She couldn't shake the dizzy feeling and the brightness of the room didn't help her shake the cobwebs on her head. It jabbed her like a sharp cue stick . . . then the sudden assault on her senses subsided.

A dark-skinned dude with wavy eyes stood beside the bed. "How are you feeling?" he asked in a soft melodic voice. He must've peeped her confusion by her expression. "Sorry. My name is Jean. My lil' brother and your lil' brother are good friends—in fact comrades, partners in crime." He tried to lighten the mood mentioning those two together.

Compton didn't have many friends. In fact, she only knew

of one. "So you are Moo-Moo's brother?" she softly and slowly said to him.

"Since the day he was born," Jean said with a warm smile. "Now"—changing the subject—"back to my original question. How do you feel?"

Her body felt like she had been run over like a Mack truck and she had a monster headache. And her mouth was so dry that it felt like she had been sucking on cotton balls.

"Awful. Like cobwebs on my head or something—can't really explain," she said, trying. Trying to explain her aches and pains was just too much energy, energy that she simply didn't have.

The smile on Jean's face stretched wider.

"Why does me feeling awful bring joy to you?" Calliope demanded to know. "And where is my brother?" She tried to rise up but the muscles in her body didn't cooperate.

"Calm down," Jean coaxed, and he moved the pillows, helping her get comfortable. "You are going to hurt yourself more than you already are." He explained. "I didn't smile because you aren't feeling well, but because *awful* is an upgrade from the condition we found you in."

He told her how, along with the plethora of scrapes and bruises, she suffered a fractured rib and a major concussion. Jean had paid a nurse to watch over her 24/7, pumping her with painkillers, tenderness, and care.

Absorbing the details of her injuries, she placed a hand on the bandage wrapped around her head and remembered the Russian, the one that slithered from the closet, Rusty's head exploding—blood and brains splattering the wall like a gory abstract painting—right in front of her very eyes. She was next. It was all coming back to her.

Calliope said, "I was shot in the head."

"No. Not shot, but hit hard with a butt of the gun, but thankfully not shot," he said, looking up to the ceiling as if he was giving thanks to the man above. "You were definitely spared."

Jean passed her a cup of water from the glass night table on the side of the bed. He placed the straw in her mouth as his hands rested on hers because he was unsure of her grip.

Room temperature, the water washed the dryness away. The liquid felt cool and refreshing going down. "They killed Rusty," she said, letting go and handing the glass back to Jean. "Why was I so lucky?"

"Being lucky had nothing to do with it. From what I could discern, somebody with very deep pockets put a green light on the head of the cop Rusty. The Russian you encountered took the contract. And in a clever way they used you to catch Rusty slipping at his own game."

She thought for a second and it did make good sense to her.

Rusty had crossed a lot of people for many years. She herself had encountered at least eight of those people who knew about the scam that he was running with Calliope. She never thought it was a real good idea—blackmailing influential men, with the threat of exposing their perverted habits, which could ultimately result in them loosing their families and livelihoods. Calliope was only sixteen—jailbait—and if a successful man was exposed he would be ruined and the effects would be detrimental.

"But why not kill me too?" Calliope asked, shaking at how close she'd come to being exterminated right alongside Rusty.

"Oh," said Jean. "There is a simple answer to that."

"All ears." Calliope waited to hear the reason.

Jean said, "The Russians, as mean and violent as they are, don't murder people for free, unless it's personal. And you weren't part of the invoice."

Miami could be as dangerous as it was glamorous, a known fact among those who lived there. But Jean made the bottom line of why Calliope didn't die with a bullet to the head sound like a mere business transaction.

Asshole! Damn, did he have to be so blunt about it?

"I hope I didn't come off as an insensitive butthole."

Too late, Calliope said to herself, and rolled her eyes.

As close to an apology as she would get, Jean said, "Sensitivity isn't one of my strong suits. Sometimes it's hard to say or show that I care, but I'm a good guy."

Before she could think about the words that Jean said, her brother entered the room, and seeing him put a smile on her face. He came over and gave her a hug and a kiss on the cheek and sat on the other side at the foot of the bed.

That's when the nurse he'd hired stormed into the room like a hurricane with dreads. Juanita, the fifth-generation healer in her family—yet, the first with formal schooling in the professional sense with a degree—was no-nonsense. She barked, "Chop! Chop!" with two swift hand claps that echoed like a whip being cracked. "Patient needs her rest," she announced. "No more company."

Protesting, Calliope said, "Can I have a few minutes with my brother before you put them out please?"

"Plenty of time for that, once you are well." Juanita fluffed the pillows and filled the water cup on the night table all at the same time it seemed. "You need your rest," she said. Then she fished a bottle of pain medication from her smock pocket.

Calliope's eyes dotted toward Jean.

Help!

Jean smirked before coming to her rescue.

"*Ahem.*" He cleared his throat after getting Juanita's attention. He said, "It's my fault for taking up all the time and she will have a few minutes with her brother."

He could feel the daggers from Juanita. Jean ignored them. After all he was the one footing the bill. To be precise, he was the one doling out the cash. Knowing that he just spoke of himself as not having the best bedside manners or sincerity, he tried to clean it up. "She only needs a couple of minutes with her brother. I think it will do them good."

Nurse Juanita's mouth was tight enough to cut glass, but she compromised. "Five minutes. Then you take medication and get rest." The hurricane left the room and Jean followed, leaving the siblings alone to talk.

Compton rocked Sean John and a cocky smile. "You look terrible," he said with the honesty and perspective of a kid brother.

"Well thank you that, that makes me feel better already," she said sarcastically. "You are no ray of sunshine yourself."

With the sibling banter exchanged and now out of the way,

they got serious. Calliope asked, "Who has been taking care of you?" She knew damn well Mabel wouldn't step up to the plate in her absence. That would have been like asking the pope to run the Nation of Islam.

If she didn't know any better, it looked like he poked out his chest. "Been taking care of myself." Compton dug into his loose-fitting jeans and came out with two palms-full of knots of money. "Doing a'ight too."

Calliope knew the implications. "When did you start selling drugs?"

The very reason she put herself in harm's way was because she wanted so much more for her brother than being a dope dealer, like graduating high school, college, and a career . . . his own family and life pleasures.

Compton sounded too sure of himself when he answered, "Long enough to get my weight up."

Not accepting the murky response, Calliope asked again. "How long?"

"A few weeks," he confessed—some of the air removed from his cocky chest this time. The interrogation far from over, she asked, where he got the drugs. Somehow, she felt she already knew the answer, but wanted to hear it straight from the horse's mouth.

Compton tried dodging the question. "Why does it matter where I score from?"

"Is it Jean?"

Tight-lipped.

But not denying the accusation was confirmation enough

for Calliope. She let out a deep sigh. "Is he forcing you to sell for him?"

"It's not like that, sis. Don't nobody and can't nobody force me to do nothing. Jean's like the big brother I never had. He holds me down and gives me advice. He holds me accountable and makes sure I'm good the same as he does for Moo-Moo."

The truth of the matter was that Jean didn't want that life for his brother either. However, what was he going to do? He tried to talk the boys out of their decision to trap, but once their minds were set in concrete, he insisted in the best way he knew how. Boys will be boys. He hoped that it would be a phase that he would grow out of.

Killing the vibe, Juanita marched back into the room. "Time's up, patient needs her rest," she said in a manner of a drill sergeant.

Locking eyes with her brother, Calliope told him, "Please be careful."

He kissed her on the forehead and, with a smile about the size of the Biscayne Bay washed over his face, said, "I got this. I got us."

13

Calliope paced the floor back and forth, watching the entryway to the door, hoping and praying that everything would fall in place. She couldn't believe that Compton had gotten himself caught up and wasn't for sure how things would turn out. Finally she saw Mabel's lime green outfit making its way through the door. Calliope exhaled before she could thank God that Mabel had finally made it there. "Where the hell is my money?" Mabel came out of her face then extended her hand with her palm up.

Calliope shot her a look and if she was anybody other than her great-grandmother by blood—and that was alleged—she would have cussed her out. But out of respect she didn't. Instead she took a deep breath, bit her tongue, counted to five, then went into her Gucci purse and handed Mabel the two hundreds and a fifty-dollar bill.

Mabel looked at the three bills as if something was wrong, and in her eyes it was. "Look, lil' girl, run me my cash. Ain't nobody got time to be playing with you. It's too early in the morning for this mess and I'm going to mess around and miss bingo down here with this foolishness here! Didn't I tell you on day one, when I picked y'all up that this was business? Now, I want the rest of my money."

Before Calliope was about to blow her top, she counted to herself again and then took more air into her lungs, locked eyes with Mabel, and said, "And you will get the rest of your money as soon as you do what *you* are supposed to do. Now that's how business work. . . . You get half now, and half when your task is completed."

Mabel stared at her for a good thirty seconds and Calliope didn't break her look either. "All right then," she said, and sucked her teeth, leaned into Calliope, and said to her in a tone above a whisper, "And I don't want no shit out of y'all some when it come to my damn money." She put her hand on her hip and was using the other to point at Calliope to let her know that she was jiving.

Calliope said, "Do what you are supposed to do then, and rest assured, it's plenty more where that came from. Now maybe you should go to the bathroom and get that lipstick off your teeth."

Mabel was a tad bit embarrassed that she had her red Revlon lipstick on her teeth. "I will do just that, and see you in court."

As Calliope made her way into the actual courtroom, the bailiff was beginning the proceeding with, "All rise."

A gavel jockey, sporting a pair of granny glasses on the tip of his nose, balding head, and gray mustache, wearing a black robe, took the stand as if he were a king among his subjects. The judge milked the moment for everything it was worth.

"You may be seated," he informed his citizens.

She copped a squat on the row bench, legs crossed at the knees. The guy beside her couldn't stop eyeballing her or her Seven jeans that were molded to her toned calves and shapely thighs. It had been over six months since her near-death experience and Calliope had recovered unblemished. In fact, her body had filled out more. At seventeen, legally she was still jailbait, but dangerously drop-dead gorgeous.

To the thirsty creep sitting next to her, she said, "Stop fish bowling me before something accidently gets stuck in your eye."

"Don't flaunt it, if you don't want it."

"Perve," followed by a slender middle finger and she was done with him.

Two cases went by before she shuffled Compton out. "Your Honor."

The prosecutor stood. "Mr. Conley, you were apprehended with five hundred and twelve baggies of crack cocaine, totaling the weight 100.6 grams. Along with one thousand dollars in cash."

This was the first time that Calliope had heard the actual accusations. The prosecutor, in her mind, was making Compton to be Nino Brown, Jr., of the South. Meanwhile in her peripheral vision, she glimpsed a familiar face among the people in the gallery. When she turned to be sure that it belonged to the person she thought it did, he winked.

Jean. Why the fuck was he here? It was all coming together. It was his fault that Compton was selling drugs in the first place anyway. Calliope's thoughts were interrupted when the judge asked, "Do you have anyone representing you, son?"

Calliope was about to stand, but a dapper, middle-aged man from the front row beat her to the punch.

"Yes, sir, Michael Weikenstein, and I'm Mr. Conley's attorney."

His appearance alone played a major part. The suit the lawyer wore was so expensive, it seemed that one would have to be either famous or a major drug kingpin to even afford his retainer.

The judge tried to disguise his surprise. "I see."

What broke out was a good old fashioned prison-yard knife fight but in a courtroom. In place of hardened convicts were two fork-tongued rival Ivy League litigators. The prosecutor had drawn first blood. Now it was time for the defense.

"First of all, Your Honor, my client is only thirteen."

"He will be fourteen in less than thirty days, Your Honor," the prosecutor interjected.

"We are not talking about thirty days, Your Honor, we are talking about today, right now at this minute."

"You have a valid point, Mr. Weikenstein."

"As I was saying before interrupted, my client is only thirteen years old and prefers to be called by his first name Compton. Mr. Conley is Compton's father, a man he hasn't seen since he was four but that's neither here nor there. I'm here to discuss the merit of the charges." The judge's gleaming head bopped up and down. "That's why we are here," the Jewish Ivy League defense lawyer said. "Yes, five hundred and twelve baggies of coke, totaling one hundred point six grams in weight was found. But not on my client. The coke was found in a drainpipe in the Pork and Beans Projects. My client lives with his great-grandma in Miami Lakes."

The prosecutor didn't take the potentially fatal blows sitting down. "Then what's he doing hanging out less than twenty feet away from the drugs in Pork and Beans Housing Projects then?"

As if he'd been waiting for the outburst, Compton's well-paid attorney said, "Visiting a friend. No crime in that. Not everyone is fortunate enough to have friends who only live in the suburbs."

Snickering in the gallery.

"And the money," the defense attorney continued as if the explanation was simple, "a gift from his great-grandmother. To go school shopping, if I may add, and get a couple of money orders for her various bills."

"How convenient," the prosecutor snorted. "I'm sure he had a reason for running from the police also."

Weikenstein flashed a set of gleaming white teeth as if he predicted that he'd be asked. "I do," he said. "He was afraid. The police in question were undercover, wearing plain clothes. My client had no way of knowing who was chasing him. The painful truth is that Pork and Beans Projects is a dangerous place at times, people sometimes run to stay alive. May I add, not being from around those parts can be even harder."

He's good, Calliope thought to herself. She wanted to stand and clap for the lawyer's performance, his final blow a coup de grâce.

"Well," the judge decided, "if the great-grandmother can vouch for the money, your client can be released to your custody. If not, it's the home."

Where the fuck is Mabel? Calliope wondered anxiously. She had been so caught up in Mr. Weikenstein's performance that she had not noticed that Mabel hadn't entered into the courtroom. Calliope knew good and well that Mabel had better not have left and been at bingo jacking off the money.

"Is there a funeral going in dis here place or something? So damn quiet." Mabel made a grand entrance into the courtroom, making the judge do a double take at her lime top, and the lime beret she had cocked to the side with a rhinestone broach in the middle of it.

The judge slammed the gavel, ordering silence in the court. "That's what I'm talking about," said Mabel. "Nothing like a bit damn little order. That's how I run my house, with order, sir."

The judge seemed flabbergasted, and confused. "Who are you, ma'am? And how may I help you?" Then he looked for the bailiff for help. She shrugged the bailiff off her.

Mabel put her hands on her hips. "I am Mabel Moon and I'm the great-grandmother of that there boy that you got all shackled up like he's some kind of criminal. It just doesn't make any kinds of sense how you people try to criminalize these kids at such a young age. Talking about y'all some want them to be multi-cultural and getting along with chill-ings from all walks of life and when they venture to the other side of town, you locks 'em up."

"Miss," he interjected. The judge pushed his granny glasses farther up his long nose. "You are the great-grandmother?"

"I just said that I was, didn't I? But I prefer to be called Two Gs Mabel." Big pockets of laughter came from the gallery.

"One question, uh, Mabel. Your great-grandson had a thousand dollars on his person," the judge stated. "Do you by any chance know where he came by that much money?"

If Mabel answered the question incorrectly, everything that the lawyer had achieved would have been out of the window. The room became devoid of oxygen as the entire courtroom waited for the answer.

Mabel asked incredulously, "A thousand dollars? Did you just say that that boy had a thousand dollars on him?"

The judge became impatient. "Yes, Ms. Moon, I did. Do you know where he could have come by so much money?"

"All I know is," Mabel said indignantly, "is that one of yo cricked-ass po-pos must of stole some of it and that just doesn't make any senses either. Judge, I'm expecting you to make them accountable. Because I gave that boy fifteen hundred before he left home, clothes these days are expensive as I don't know what. Can't get nearly nothing anymore, then the gas bill, light bills, I mean Power and Lights, someone need to do something about that. I try to pay on time; my feet bad and I can't stand in those lines because my two dogs hurt me so bad. That's why I'm Two Gs Mabel, you heard me?"

Pandemonium broke out. People couldn't stop laughing, the bailiffs cracking up themselves.

"Order in the court." The judge wanted the laughter to come to a halt, but was trying to hold his own in.

Then the prosecutor spoke up, "Now what about the curfew charge because he was out after one in the morning."

Before Mr. Weikenstein could get his two cents in, the judge ruled. "Mr. Conley will be released to Ms. Two Gs Mabel Moon and an ankle bracelet will be placed on his ankle until his fifteenth birthday to ensure that he will be in the house every day before dark, unless with his great-grandmother."

Once outside the courtroom, Mabel collected her other two fifty and announced that she was late for bingo and hoped they had bus fare home.

Calliope watched as Jean shook Compton's attorney's hand. She waited for Jean to finish up with the attorney before she approached Jean.

"Hello, gorgeous." He gave her a kiss on the cheek. His cologne was something special to smell. The aroma screamed rich.

"Listen, thank you for the attorney and all that but at the same time, I don't want Compton caught up in your," she said in a whisper, "drug enterprise."

"It's not what you think."

"Cut the bullshit with me."

"Can I take you to dinner so we can talk it over?"

"Nothing to talk about," she shot back at him, then realized that she should probably humble herself a little because Jean had been a lifesaver—hers at that. "Listen, I thank you for helping my brother rescue me, and for you having Juanita the nurse take care of me. I'm so grateful to you, and this attorney, he was really a class act. But I need you to understand that my brother is all I have. And he has his whole life in front of him and I don't want him caught up in the system and throwing his life away."

"I understand and agree totally."

"Then why then?" she asked.

"I promise you I feel the same way about my little brother, but the two of them once they put their heads together and decide to do something, it's nothing nobody can do to stop them. You know that."

She knew what he was saying was true about Moo-Moo and Compton. She only nodded in agreement.

"So, all I do is try to accommodate what they are going to do and make sure they are not in harm's way. Now what I'm thinking what we can do is stay in touch, compare notes, and this way we are not sideswiped when it comes to those two."

"You are so right."

"If you don't mind, I'm going to call you and swing by on a regular. Is that okay?" Jean asked.

"Fine by me."

For the hours it took for them to process the necessary paperwork for Compton's release, Jean kept her company. The two went for lunch and then came back, and the procedure turned into an all-day process, but getting acquainted with her new friend made time fly. Before they knew it, Compton was finally home and settled. Though Jean had left Compton with some cash, Compton still had a long look on his face. "What's wrong Comp?"

"Just wondering what we going to do for money, now that I'm on this house arrest bullshit."

"Don't worry about that. I will come up with something. Don't I always?"

14

Calliope opened up the mailbox and saw the letter from the Florida Board of Education. She couldn't help but to rip it open, and there it was: she was in possession of her GED. She was overjoyed and couldn't wait to tell Jean. Before she was back in the door good, she had grabbed her phone to call Jean to tell him of the good news. He was happy and said four words, "This calls for celebration."

Jean and her had been together over nine months now. In the beginning, he tried to convince her to stop dancing and he would take care of her, but she would hear nothing of it.

Then he came up with a better plan: if she took GED classes, he'd give her an allowance so that she wouldn't have to be up all night working and could focus on school. So this was just as much of his accomplishment as it was hers.

For the first time in her life, things were going great. Compton was attending a good school, making Bs and excelling to the top of his class. He was voted best dressed. Though Compton hated the fact that she was seeing Jean, he couldn't mind too much since he wasn't any of those dirty old men that Rusty had her scamming, and at least Jean kept her off the pole.

The relationship between Calliope and Jean was growing and the two were inseparable. Shortly after court, Mabel had a stroke and Calliope stepped up to the plate to take care of her. She was appreciative to Calliope and realized that Calliope was the only family that she had. She couldn't believe that things were finally looking up.

Jean had come over to take Calliope and Compton to dinner to celebrate. He was proud and very happy for her but she could tell that it was something heavy on his mind. After they got back from dinner, she asked him, "Is everything all right, baby?"

He didn't give her a straight answer. Instead he asked, "So, do you love me?"

"Yes," she quickly said not even having to think. "You know I do. Why would you ask me such a stupid question anyway?"

He ignored her question and then asked her another question. "How much?"

"A whole lot." Her eyes confirmed as they lit up.

He wanted to believe her, but he simply said, "Okay, we will see."

"And just how do you plan to measure my love?" she asked, interested to know the details of his measuring cup.

"Time, baby . . . only time will tell."

"Okay," she said, wanting to go into depth but not rustle his feathers. She knew him well, and was sure that he was going somewhere with his line of questioning. Where? She didn't know but knew he'd reveal it soon. She reminded him, "Whenever you are ready to talk, you know I'm here for you."

"Look, real talk, baby girl, been wanting to talk to you about something for a few days now but didn't know how to, but I'm going to just put my cards on the table."

She was puzzled when she observed the look of seriousness on his face. "Baby, what is it?" she asked as sympathetic as she could.

He was quiet for a few minutes and then she fell into his arms. "Baby, talk to me, you know whatever is on your mind is safe with me."

He searched her face and all he saw was sincerity. He shook his head. Calliope grabbed his hand. "Talk to me, baby," she insisted.

"Man, you know how when shit is going good, shit just be too good."

"I know that feeling, I'm feeling it now, finally after all the stuff I have been through. But we solid, right?" she asked.

"Depends," he said.

"On?" she asked, wanting him to just let it all out what exactly "depends" meant.

"On how you deal with it. Only you will be able to keep us on solid ground."

"Stop talking in circles and share what's on your mind. Just kick it, for real."

"It's like this: I got to go turn myself in and do nine months on this assault charge."

"When?" she asked.

"In two days."

She was quiet for a few minutes. "Okay. Can't you call me?"

"I can call."

"And I can come and visit, right?"

"I get visits. But I don't want to get my hopes up high of you saying you going to come, and I go get a haircut, up ready for my visit with you and you don't show up, having me look crazy and all that shit. I ain't on that kind of bullshit." She tried to cut him off.

"I would never—"

But he continued with his tangent.

"Seen it too many times. That's what chicks say in the beginning. They would be there and then things change gradually."

She became offended and felt that she needed not only to put him in place but also take up for herself. "Look, it's like this. I ain't never had much of shit, but through all the things I went through, I always reminded myself that those things didn't affect who I was and one day I'd be the shit. And I've always believed that if my word ain't shit then I ain't shit. And me not being the shit in any aspect of the word, isn't happening." She locked eyes with him. "So I said, I'd ride these nine months with you and that's what I plan to do."

He gazed in her eyes and saw nothing but love, concern, and sincerity. She wasn't sure if it was the intense way he looked at her or the realness of the conversation that made her want to cry. The fact of the matter was her friend, her confidant, her boo, the guy who owned her heart and the man she had lost her virginity to was going to be physically removed from her for the next nine months. She tried like hell to hold back her tears to be strong for him, and he could see the water in her eyes and that's when he was convinced and took her in his arms.

When he did, she whispered, "I will be there for you faithfully, while you do them nine months. . . . I promise."

15

Calliope definitely didn't make any promises just to break them. She held up her end of the bargain. She went to visit every single visiting day, wrote letters and sent cards practically every day. When he called she was always available for his phone calls. It did help that he had left her ten grand to take care of her and Compton, and his boy Jacques was supposed to bring her money weekly, which in the beginning he did and after a month or so after her ten grand ran out, Jacques changed his number.

"What the hell you mean, this motherfucker avoiding you?" Jean asked from the other side of the glass in the visitation room.

"My friend Casha told me that Jacques was in Lil Haiti and I went down there to see him."

"Okay . . . and. He came off that paper right?"

"Not hardly, baby. The minute he saw my car bend the corner was the minute that he disappeared around the next corner."

"Two minutes, until visits over," the guard running visitation said.

"Here write these numbers down, and call these folks. They owe me money too," he said to her before saying their goodbyes. "Call you later on tonight, baby."

When she got in the car, she began to start making the calls and the clowns started giving her the runaround, talking about how they were going to call her back. As she put her car in reverse, she caught a glance of herself in the rearview mirror, and then she got a call, a wake-up call from herself, with a strong message.

Listen . . . what the fuck you doing? she asked herself, then told herself, *You must be out your rabbit-ass mind acting just like Shelly. You around here depending on a nigga . . . to figure out shit for you, to make sure you and Compton got y'all next meal. Bitch, is you crazy? You don't chase nobody for no nigga's money—or wait for no nigga to break you off when he sees fit. You get own money— always have and always will. Now make yo money! That's who you are, and that's what you do.*

Though she faithfully kept the visits coming and letters pouring in, she did what she did . . . kept her word to her man and got *her* money!

16

The Double Life

The cocaine-white drop-top Mercedes cruised up and stopped smack dead in front of the club at 10:15 P.M. The real action didn't take off until well after midnight but Cinnamon always liked showing up early, to get a feel for the crowd and to observe exactly where the money was.

From the passenger seat, she grabbed her Chanel purse and Gucci overnight bag, then slid out of her whip. "Take care of my baby." She flashed a smile to Tony, the head valet attendant and the guy who always opened the door and helped her out of the car. She gave him a big smile along with a twenty.

"Thanks, Cinnamon." Tony winked. "American Airlines ain't got nuttin' on yo fly ass. You do know I'm single, right?" He was always flirting, hoping one day that she'd take him up on his offer.

"You've only told me about a thousand times," she said. "Don't forget to put the top up for me, baby." She loved riding at night with the roof back. It was just something about the wind whipping through her long Brazilian weave that cleared her mind and made her feel free.

"You got it, Your Flyness."

The entire club's movement of making money was achieved by the same principles of a Super Bowl–winning football team working as one. The valet's responsibility began with getting the customers inside quickly, so that the offense could go to work relieving them of their do-re-mi.

"What's up, Cinnamon?" The bouncer annoyed a few that were waiting in line when he allowed her to skip the line and rushed her in.

Inside, compared to a lot of the bigger-named spots, didn't meet expectations, décor wise.

She often thought about how deceiving this place could be—glamorous on the outside, but a hole-in-the-wall inside. That didn't stop either the patrons from coming or the workers from making that paper by the boatload, though.

Booty shaking was always in the full effect, almost around the clock, twenty-three hours out of the day.

Half-dressed, buck-naked daughters and baby mamas—most sporting at least one variation of pierced pussies, inflamed-asses from bootleg butt shots, or huge breast implants—strutted their stuff throughout the club. The circled stage, with three tall poles where at least two or three chicks performed at all times, danced for tips. The bartenders, all women, all hot, made great drinks and better tips, and were usually either retired dancers or girls who auditioned to strip and didn't make the cut.

By 1:30 the VIP room was turned all the way up. As for

broads the ballers were checking for to make it rain on them, Cinnamon had that part on lock. She was hands down the most popular dancer there. In her zone, she took the art of pussy popping to another level. Sexy. Limber. And in complete control of all her body parts. Dancing came natural to her and seducing anybody male or female with her eyes was second nature to her.

Other chicks (dancers and civilians alike) shot nasty, envious glares at her but that never intimidated her. Hating don't make dollars or sense, she thought with a winning smirk, watching weak-willed men show their appreciation for her talents with mountains of one-dollar, twenty-dollar, fifty-dollar, and hundred-dollar bills. There was no denying money floated like confetti when she took the main stage and not to mention when she made an entrance to the VIP room.

A light layer of perspiration coated her well-toned body from the intensity of her dancing and demonstration of her contortionist abilities. Time for a costume change, she thought as she was about to make her way to the dressing room.

That's when she seen him. She couldn't believe her eyes. She had only taken her daily shot to the head to jump-start her night off and a twelve-hour energy drink, so she wasn't drunk. Had she caught some kind of contact from all the weed smoke that filled the air and her mind was playing tricks on her?

"What the fuck?" were the words that ran through her mind but verbally the same words that came out of Jean's mouth when he seen her half-naked coming out of the VIP room. Her seductive smile that she wore quickly turned to fear. She felt like she had been caught doing something she had no business doing, and in Jean's eyes she had. She didn't know how to react or what to say. "What the hell you doing here?" she asked Jean.

"I could ask the same thing." He shot back almost speechless.

"I'm working. When did you get out?"

He looked her up and down in total disgust and then smacked the shit out of her, making her stumble down the three steps that led up to the VIP room. He then leaned down and said, "Since you want to act like a whore, fuck and shit. I'm going to treat you as such."

"What?" she said, trying to gather herself, her pride, and her heart off of the floor. "A whore?" she questioned.

"Yeah, you in VIP fucking and shit," he said putting his hands around her neck.

"I swear on everything I love, that's the farthest from the truth."

"Shut the fuck up. I don't want to hear it." He silenced her with his fingers and broke her feelings. The truth of the matter was she did dance for money, but that's it. Danced. No sex, no prostitution. Now did a lot of girls in the club exchange sex for money? Absolutely, but not her. She learned a long time ago that as long as she danced and didn't make sex an option, the patrons would always come back and spend money, in hopes that one day, someday, they would get lucky. And they never did, not the funniest, not the cutest, not the wealthiest. No matter what he thought or said, the fact still remained that he was still the only man she had had sex with.

"I got out today, on some good behavior shit. I had to meet somebody here to get some money that belongs to me and was on my way to come surprise you, but I guess since you been giving the pussy away acting like a whore, I guess I will go give this good dick away!" he said to her. "I should've known better. I met you whoring. And I was taught that you can never turn a whore into a housewife!"

By now she was in tears, and Mocha had come over to comfort her. She tried to fight the tears back but by the time she got to the dressing room, she was crying a waterfall. She hated that the other dancers saw her crying, but, shit, she was only human. She couldn't figure out what hurt her the most, that Jean hit her or that he called her a whore.

17

In the Heart of Downtown Richmond, Virginia

A light rain drizzled from an uptight, overcast sky, as urban dwellers, many just getting off of the daily grind, scurried about Broad Street trying to keep from getting too wet. A couple blocks west of the newly built federal court building—inside a barbershop called The Chop Shop—cats were not only staying dry but also holding court amongst friends.

Lynx, a once big-time hustler who was still respected in the city, owned the shop. It was equipped with a dozen skilled barbers—with clientele consisting of a lot of Richmond's underworld and reformed drug dealers turned working men—four fifty-inch flat screens, an ambient surround sound system, and a wet bar. The Chop Shop was the coldest spot in the city to get not only a fresh cut but the latest news in the streets or in the penitentiary, tight gear, new electronics, and Vegas-style odds on major sporting events. Or just chop it up about who is making bread and who's only trimming the crust. As customary,

The Chop Shop was packed, believe it or not the damp weather had no impact on business or the old-school social networking.

Pope, one of the regulars, took a shot at Lynx. He said, "Been meaning to ask you something. Why da fuck you cop a barbershop and you don't know shit about cutting hair?"

A few cats laughed.

Pope was a rare dude, a well respected OG, who'd earned his stripes in the game and survived to reap a lot of the rewards and benefits. Pope had never seen the inside of a prison, and he never dropped two nickels on anyone. These things—for the streets—were as atypical as a Catholic *not* being fond of young boys. "In my day," Pope added, "cats didn't start a business that they couldn't finish, if need be."

Another one of the regulars, excitedly said, "He got ya right there, Lynx," and nodded his head.

Pope made a solid point, Lynx thought: an owner that couldn't perform the job (regardless of what the job entailed) was at the mercy of his employees. Kind of like a pimp with his whores.

Normally, Lynx held the role of adjudicator in the shop's debate, but every now and again, he had to defend himself. Half the eyes in the shop, and two-thirds the ears honed in on Lynx. A man's ability to hustle said a lot about him and Lynx's hustle had been put on trial. He had no choice but to defend himself and his actions.

Cucumber cool, with none of the greenness, Lynx brushed away a speck of imaginary dusk from his Versace button-up. The fifteen-hundred-dollar shirt was a present from his wife. With eyes on him, as thorough as high-tech surveillance cameras, he took a sip of tequila, one of the perks of being the boss and not having to shave or cut heads: he could drink on the job. Then he smiled a little and agreed. "I see the logic in what you are saying Pope. And it's legit . . . in theory. But in practice, your view lacks imagination."

While cats were stirring the pot between Lynx and Pope, the wind blew a peddler into the shop. "I got all flavor roses for the low-low," the flower hustler made the grand announcement to the shop, with a few samples of his product in hand and the rest of them were outside in the van, double-parked in front of the shop.

Always wanting to patronize another man's grind, Lynx bought four dozen. Red. Thirty-six for his wife, Bambi, and twelve for their daughter Nya. " 'Preciate that my man."

The flower hustler put the money in his pocket and gave Lynx a warm smile. "No doubt. Anybody else?"

A few other cats copped buds for their boos while Lynx continued to impart wisdom on Pope. "The way I see it. The strongest, the smartest, nor the man with a certain skill set is the one that rises to the top." Lynx had it mouse quiet in that place, every ear was open as he pleaded his case. "That top spot is going to always be reserved for the man with the best ideas. Because it's the ideas that make the bread," Lynx said.

"Preach!" Somebody shouted, cheering him on.

A mock applause from Pope, Lynx nodded: game acknowledging game.

Patrons of The Chop Shop continued to debate while Lynx made his way to his private office for a quick meeting.

The meeting was with a local bookie named Popcorn. Lynx

said, "Put two grand on the Lakers to cover against San Antonio. And another two on Dallas to cover over the Clippers."

Gambling was the only vice that Lynx had. He had always dabbled a little with dice, lottery tickets, and made a few wagers on a game here and there when he was in the streets heavy. But then he had plenty of money coming in to cover his bets—so if he lost it was no sweat off of his back. Then money was no obstacle. His wife had a lucrative party planning business that catered to the upper echelon, and he was knee-deep in dealing some of the best dope the city had ever saw. Nowadays he wasn't starving, but since he went legit, the money didn't come as fast as it once did and when he took a hit with the bets, it stung harder.

"Roger that. But I'm going to need that 30k you already bleeding," Popcorn informed him.

"You know I'm good for it Corn." Lynx had been on a losing streak, but that's why they called it gambling. Win some, lose some. The game was to do more winning than the latter.

"I fucks wit you, Lynx. You know I do." Popcorn looked like it hurt him to deliver the message. He took a deep breath and then tried to speak with sincerity. "But I'm just the middleman here. My boss only believes what he sees, and right now he ain't seeing the money."

Thirty k.

"I'll have all that little bread in two weeks, maybe sooner. But I'm going to need my line of credit to stay open until then. Okay?"

He and Popcorn had known each other for a real long time. They both went to John F. Kennedy High School together and played on the football team.

Popcorn looked him in the eyes and firmly said, "It's not Okay. That two weeks shit is dead—you got one, and no more credit until the books are clean. We clear?"

I guess business trumps friendship, Lynx thought but said, "Crystal."

"One more thing," said Popcorn, "and this isn't on me . . ."

"Just spit it out, Popcorn,"

Popcorn had a lump in his throat, "My boss says, to let you know, that the late penalty—that's if one has to be applied—will involve blood."

"You threatening me, Popcorn?" Lynx kept a Smith and Wesson .45 in his desk drawer and he wasn't feeling the words spilling from his "supposed" friend's mouth.

Popcorn, far from slow, felt a rise in temperature. "Never that," he quickly corrected. "I'm only the messenger. I will never personally push anything at you. But Lynx . . . As a friend, I do want you to know that these dudes are serious about what they say. I have seen them really do some horrific shit. And they're even more serious about their money. So get these people their bread—'cause man oh man! It could get bad—real bad."

Later that night . . .

"Okay, Lynx, what's wrong?" Bambi asked while they were lying in bed with the television on. Bambi was wearing a provocative Asian see-everything nightie, looking hella-sexy. Lynx barely noticed. Bambi playfully shoved him, almost knocking Lynx out of the king-size four-poster bed. "I'm talking to you," she said, when he shot her that puzzled look of his.

Nikki Turner

"You have been preoccupied with something all night. I might as well have went out tonight and ate alone, because you were there in body only. I'm still trying to figure out what planet your mind was on."

Bambi was absolutely right. Lynx couldn't get the seriousness of the conversation with Popcorn out of his mind. Now that shit had bled into his bedroom. "I'm sorry baby. You are absolutely right." He kissed her on the mouth, but she didn't reciprocate.

Bambi said, "You're not getting off that easy." Their daughter was fast asleep in the room next to theirs, so she kept her voice down. "Now, are you going to tell me what's wrong, or do I have to resort to violence?"

His wife wasn't smiling. The fact of the matter was that Bambi was even more beautiful when she got mad, and that was no easy task. "No violence unless it involves handcuffs," Lynx said playfully.

"I'm serious, Lynx. What is it?"

It wasn't easy, but Lynx had no real choice. He couldn't handle the stress alone, and he knew that his wife would have the answers. He told her about the money he owed from his gambling endeavors. After he had shared everything with her, he felt like a real chump. When he and Bambi first met, $20,000.00 was lunch money for him. That was before he'd done those three years in Club Fed. Now, although The Chop Shop was making its fair share of cheddar, in addition to the money his other businesses were bringing in, truth be told, Bambi's party planning company, Events R Us, had turned Bambi into the primary breadwinner.

"I don't want to sound like I'm preaching," Bambi said. The first infamous words before a person started preaching, "but you really need to slow down with the gambling." Lynx was about to debate his vice, when she said, "Normally, I wouldn't care if you bet us out of house and home, I would still love you. But it's not just us that we have to look out for. We have a three-year old child. We have to think about Nya. You know this," she said with passion and conviction.

How could a man argue with a woman who will sacrifice everything because she believes in her man, right or wrong? If there was a way to win the argument, Lynx didn't have it.

"I don't deserve you," he said.

Bambi told him that he could take the $20,000 from their savings account. "Don't be stupid," she said. "We deserve each other."

Lynx kissed her, and this time she kissed him back and then pulled away. "You forget something."

"What?"

Lynx had a massive hard-on poking from his boxers. Bambi just looked at him; the look was enough. He said, "I promise."

18

From out of the gate, Calliope and the manager of the club had never really seen eye to eye anyway, which didn't make it too difficult for him to fire her on the spot. No dancer with a steady clientele wanted to deal with the headache of moving clubs and possibly losing loyal clients and having to learn the personalities of the other dancers, not to mention adjust to not only the politics but also the poli-tricks of a new club.

In some kind of weird way, she was totally fine with losing her job at the club. After all, she knew too much of the same thing sometimes wasn't good. On the drive home she began to think how the long nights trickling to the early mornings, sleeping most of the days away, were getting the best of her. She felt she needed to spend some time at home anyway. . . . She just didn't really know how much of her home life had fallen by the wayside.

When she walked into the house, an hour earlier than normal, she was greeted with Compton coming down the hall heading into her bedroom with the Dr. Scholl's foot bath massager in his hand filled with water. Though he despised the kind of work she did, on the nights that she worked, when she got home, just like clockwork, Compton always had the foot bath set up for her to soak her feet. She greatly appreciated it because the heels that she wore at work were not kind to her feet, that was for sure.

While he hopped in the shower, she made breakfast for the two of them so they could chat before he left to go to school. He loved his sister's cooking more than anything. After he made his way out of the door something hit her. It was like a lightbulb went off in her head when she realized just how that vampire life had taken over her life so much and how the reality of it was that Compton was knee-deep in the streets by now.

All day he was on her mind. She had no idea what to do about it, knowing good and well that trying to manhandle him was damn near impossible. He stood well over six feet tall and had been working out and his body was cut; though not yet legal in age, he looked like a grown man.

Compton was too far-gone, and though she bitched, hollered, screamed, and tried to talk to him until she was purple in the face, there was nothing that could be done. When he came in from school, she didn't even waste her time on the small pleasantries. She held no punches and shot straight from the hip.

"Look, do you want to go to penitentiary or die in them streets? I mean let me know, so I can know how to prepare," she shot at him, and kept on going before he could digest the words she had just shoved down his throat. "You think you going to live forever and count money forever. It don't work like that. That ain't how this life you living go."

"I know it don't," he said, not really wanting to hear the perils of the game. Besides he was well aware of the seriousness. Instead he shifted the weight, wanting her to understand that his sins wasn't worse than hers either. "But I don't want you shaking your ass for them dirty ma'fuckers either," he shot back at her. "How do you think that makes me feel?"

"I feel you but that's what pays the bills, and keeps us afloat."

"Then if that's what's going to keep the lights on, I will keep doing what I do in the dark," he said to her, his voice getting deeper by the day it seemed. "Look, this was the hand we were dealt. We can ignore it and sugarcoat this shit all we want but guess what? The real is ain't nobody going to give us shit, we do what we have to do. You done almost been killed doing this shit and it's just not your place to be the man of the house. I'm old enough, and I got the means, the will, and the resources. I can hold this shit down. Let me be the man." He looked about five inches down at her.

"Selling drugs and throwing bricks at the penitentiary doesn't make you the man."

"Well I rather risk it all then have you continue being a dollar ho." He didn't realize how those words cut his sister until after they rolled off his tongue.

"So, you wanna hit me below the belt, huh?" she said, taking what he said under the chin and then defending herself. "That doesn't make what you do better. Besides, I'm not prostituting myself or breaking the law. You can go to jail for years if you get caught," she reminded him.

"No you not prostituting yourself but that shit is degrading and not what I want for you."

"You think this is what I want for myself?" She was offended by what he said, raising her voice.

"I don't think this is what you want. I think you love the money, and it makes you feel secure."

She didn't object to what her brother was saying because there was some truth in the matter. "You may have a point there. The money does help ease my pain and troubles. It ensures that we have a roof over our head and that we have plenty of options for things that we were never afforded from our parents or anyone else for that matter and in a strange way it makes me feel empowered," she had to admit.

"I know, and that's real. However, that club life." He shook his head. "It ain't safe. It dangerous in all ways." Compton was talking like the big brother. Over the past three years he'd seen so much and had grown wiser than his sixteen years.

"Listen, Comp, I know you hate what I do, but I promise I'm not going to make a career out of it. I just need to stack more money, that's all. I promise you this isn't going to be my future. I'm going to get out and do something with myself. I promise you this. I do. I really do."

Observing the tears in her eyes, he didn't want to go in any harder on her because he knew that the words he had said did have some kind of effect on her. He hugged her. "I love you! I really do," he said in her ear. "I believe you, but are you trying to convince me or yourself?"

19

For the next couple of weeks Calliope moped around the house, in her feelings. She felt like she had lost her best friend, and she had. She tried to call Jean a few times to explain but he wouldn't accept a call from her. Up until now she had never known the feeling of a real heartbreak from a man other than her father, which really didn't count. Calliope couldn't take much more of being forwarded straight to voice mail. Instead, she decided to redirect her attention back to work and focus on making her money, and a whole lot of it.

It took only her one phone call and about fifteen minutes before she had another job at a bigger and better place. She was so focused on her hustle that the only song she played in her car to and from work to remind her what her mind-set needed to be while at work and why she danced anyway was Junior M.A.F.I.A.'s "Get Money."

Club Imagination was a new club that had been opened by a man who went by the name Jiggilo. He was a seasoned veteran to the strip club world. He had been an owner of strip clubs for as long as anybody could remember. His father was a laid-back guy who ran numbers and was infamous in the gentlemen club and nightlife arena in the '60s. He was infamous for his underground titty bars and juke joints for a few decades. His wife and Jiggilo's mother, Madame Lorraine, God bless her soul, was a dance-hall dancer, turned showgirl, turned housemother, and ultimately a madame. The rumor had it that no one, man or woman, could pimp a whore like Madame Lorraine. Even some of the baddest pimps fell in line to be taken under her wing. The most flamboyant, loudest, most talkative, guttsiest woman, she had no fear in her heart whatsoever. The dame wouldn't hesitate to smack a bitch to the ground and wasn't afraid to shoot a man down with her deuce-deuce that she carried in her bosom.

In spite of that she was dedicated to the life she and her husband had laid out. However, the minute she laid eyes on Jiggilo, she knew that she didn't want her son to have any part of the life that he was born into. So the minute he was ready to embark on his elementary education, she demanded that he be sent away to be educated at one of the top boarding schools in the country. She had no problem finagling to get him admitted into the best schools that money could buy. No matter the year, time, or date, it always remained that pussy was power and one of her trusted johns knew somebody who knew somebody and just like that Jiggilo was in.

Jiggilo's father, on the other hand, Herb, was elated to have a son. After trying over twenty years to conceive a child with Lorraine, once she found out she was pregnant she started a laundry list of conditions of how their child would be raised.

At first she suggested that they would sell the business because she was adamant that she didn't want her son exposed to that life. It sounded like a good idea at first, but Herb was a long way from being a fool. With so much money pouring in, Herb stood up for the sake of his family and livelihood. He made Lorraine see that he wasn't selling his cash cow until it was close to being out of milk and she wasn't giving up her whores either. The compromise was Jiggilo would be sent away to school and allowed to visit on breaks and holidays, most of which they would spend every second of taking him on vacations, making up for lost time. There was no doubt that Jiggilo knew that his parents loved him, and the older they got, they were positive they had made the right decision.

Herb hated the thought of sending his only child and son away but knew better to rock the boat when it came to Lorraine and the child that she went through thirty-six hours of labor with and almost died giving birth to. That son of hers was her everything and she protected him with her all.

It was Herb's dream to pass the family business over to his son. It hurt him to his heart that his son would never be a part of what he had built from the ground up, so the one thing he did was to give his son the name Jiggilo.

Jiggilo went off to school, and excelled. He became a first-class gentleman, with class, charm, charisma, and good looks. He made his mother proud. However, the very thing she fought tooth and nail to keep him from was the same exact thing that he ran to and embraced with opened arms . . . the adult entertainment world.

Once he was done with his master's degree in business, he

took over his father's business, and within the next ten years he had a chain of adult toy stores and his hands in twelve major clubs across the United States, not to mention the massive-production-style strip clubs under his belt in just about every major city in the United States. As the years went on and he gained more knowledge from trial and error, these numbers grew. Every one of this clubs was an entire experience. His vision alone was light-years ahead of the other clubs and enabled him to corner the market and monopolize the industry. He concentrated on every little detail of the designs, décor, and politics. After all, no one could deny that he had his mother's flamboyance and opulence, and his newest club, Imagination Cabaret, did not disappoint.

Everybody flocked to Club Imagination, once a warehouse turned into a heaven where patrons could let their imagination run wild, and even then the experience was still beyond anything the average or the extraordinary could imagine. It had one huge room filled with waterfalls resembling Niagara Falls with women playing in the water. While on the other side, there were volcanos that erupted with lava. Then another part featured palm trees and neon lights. The place had rapidly become legendary. People came from all around to experience the Imagination lifestyle. It was the home to the most seductive, exotic-looking, and talented dancers on the planet, and this without a doubt included Calliope aka Cinnamon.

Since she had started working there only six weeks ago, not only had she paid her car off, she signed the contract on a lease-to-own condo. Surprisingly she had already stacked almost a hundred Gs and this was only from working the day shift.

Tonight was her first night on the night shift. She only prayed that the night shift would be as good and lucrative to her as the day shift had faithfully been. Though she knew the competition there would be a little stiffer. That was to be expected. Since there was more money coming through at night, the girls were more catty. That wasn't intimidating to her at all—she didn't need any new friends anyway. She was there for one reason and one reason only, to get her money, stack her paper, and go home. Now if she was able to pick up a couple of good friends on the way, then that would be splendid, but if not then so be it. Needless to say she was definitely ready to see what the night had in store for her.

Once she arrived, she signed in and paid her fee to the housemother so that she could dance. She took the first thirty minutes and observed the dancers and the customers before she changed out and hit the floor. She had to admit it was some stiff competition and some badass chicks that was strutting their stuff through the place. At first she wondered if she'd be able to compete but then she reminisced on what Mocha had told her. "Look, if you gonna do this, it's rules to this shit! No drugs, no alcohol. I don't care what other chicks are doing. Stay away. It's going to always be your downfall. You gotta know who you are . . . you are a bad bitch, and you are in control. Be aggressive, be firm, stand your ground. Know what you will and won't do, and don't waver from that. You being a new face equals new money. And the more you don't fuck the better your luck. Stroke and cater to these niggas' egos and they will give you everything they got plus what they can't afford to. Got it."

Once she ran Mocha's words through her head a few times,

her alter-ego took over. She checked her makeup in the mirror
one last time and her game face was looking back. That's all she
needed to motivate and inspire her. She took the floor and
before she knew it, the club was hers. Two hours flew by and
she had been dancing nonstop and was sweaty and prayed that
she hadn't reached the point of musty yet.

Still with a one-track mind, she headed to the dressing room
for an outfit change that she felt she so desperately needed when
someone grabbed her hand. It was him, her "Big Spender aka
her Papi Chulo," she called him.

A smile took over Calliope's face; there was no hiding that
she was surprised to see him but glad he had found her. This
handsome guy had been coming in the club every single day,
faithfully, for the past week while she was on day shift and he
seemed to only have eyes for her. Though physical appearance
really meant nothing to her, because if the paper was right,
she'd entertain Kermit the Frog. He was dapper, tall, slim, and
light-skinned, and an official baller status. He was indeed her
preference, and, with that being said, he had nothing in common
with the Muppets.

The for-sure thing about the club atmosphere is the girls
smelled the money—and his aroma had a few other dancers
approaching him for a dance. But he turned them all down
looking for Cinnamon, and the minute he grabbed her hand
she saw green-eyed envy of the other dancers.

"Hey, you," he said to her.

She gave him the biggest smile. "Hey, babes!" she said,
fanning herself, trying to cool off.

"Why you didn't tell me they changed your work schedule?" he asked.

"They called me this morning and told me, and I didn't have a way to tell you."

"Well, we gotta change that," he said.

She never really passed her phone number along to her patrons, but it seemed that this was different. She didn't want to break her rule but at the same time she didn't act on his request right at that moment.

He placed his arms around her waist, wanting to bring her in closer to him.

"Papi Chulo, I'm sweaty as hell." She leaned in and said over the loud music, "Don't wanna get your casket-sharp clothing sweaty. So, let me change my clothes, then I'm all yours," she teased, batting her long eyelashes. Then passively asked, "Is that okay?"

He smiled. "Cool. That's what I like about you. You about your bread, but you ain't greedy and you want to make sure you handle your shit proper. I like that." He said he'd wait on her in the "Big Spenders'" room. "Rosé cool for me to order for you?" he asked.

"Perfect, baby," she said, and rubbed his cheek and promised to return right away. Normally she would have never left his side, but she knew she had the fact that he'd turned down others on her side.

Cinnamon usually would've taken at least a twenty-five to forty-five-minute break between performances and outfit changes, but she wasn't trying to give any of those thirsty, bloodsucking hoodrats-on-the-prowl a chance to beat her for her cheddar, so she took care of her business quick fast and in a hurry and was back out in ten. Wet-wiped. Ho bathed in the quickest way. Perfumed. Fresh outfit. Check, check, check.

Papi Chulo shooed the hovering vultures away when he saw her step in. Her seven-inch high heels stabbed the floor like daggers in the other girls' hearts. *Too bad, bitches,* she thought, smiling and strutting her way past the other dancers while she made eye contact with him and never seemed to lose it as she successfully navigated the high-end crowd, dodging propositions and confessions of love at first sight. She stopped at the corner table where he was.

Papi Chulo aka Big Spender gave her an approving once over. She could tell that he was indeed pleased with her skimpy, bright orange, custom-designed costume hugging and biting in all the right peaks and valleys.

"Well worth the wait," he complimented.

"Thank you, baby." She smiled.

Calliope had gotten in good with the right people from the first day she started at Club Imagination. She and the DJ had a good understanding, and he liked that she played fair. She had previously tipped the DJ nicely to put on one of her favorite songs from her playlist that she provided him. Though she didn't do drugs, music was her drug. This is why she always paid the jockey well to keep in mind her favorite jams as he spinned the records.

Calliope's perfectly shaped ass started swaying to the beat of the music and then started to act as if it was operating to its own marching orders. She had Big Spender mesmerized and almost automatically he started peeling that paper off to her. She continued and dropped it to the floor, backed up on him, and made it pop like she was epileptic.

Her moves were unpredictable, hot, and quickly sparked a flame in the Big Spender's pants and his pockets.

The heat-seeking missile in his pants prepared for takeoff, and he wanted more. "Sorry, fella, but dancing is all you get," she said, but still kept dancing for him.

The harder he got, it seemed, the more generous he became. By the third song, he was throwing money like it was rice at a wedding.

Raising her leg, Cinnamon placed a foot with open-toed, laced-up heels beside him on the chair. Her pedicure was candy-apple polish, freshly done and sexy as hell.

He sucked in a breath.

Inhaling the aroma of the coochie just three-inches from his nose made his eyes roll in ecstasy. A spritz of Flowerbomb with the natural heat of her womb was a seductive allure.

Seeing the unmitigated lust in his eyes, Cinnamon gyrated her hips so close to his face, if he was to stick out his tongue, he'd have gotten a mouthful of her G-string. He was sprung . . . and she hadn't even got loose yet.

More money than she could keep track of and four songs deep the DJ continued to rock her preselected music because he knew that one thing about Cinnamon was she was going to always make sure that he was taken care of on the back end too. If she did well, he'd do good. So, he saw to it that he played his position.

On came one of those high-testosterone tracks the dancers

in the club loved because dudes usually lost their minds trying to outdo one another when they heard the verse and the chorus.

Her trance was interrupted a little but she never gave any of her attention to them as far as her Big Spender could tell.

"Party over here!" Some other hustlers, obviously new to the Big Spenders' room, yelled from across the floor. She hated when the dudes in the club danced harder than the dancers. But she knew these kinds were simply begging for attention. She smiled thinking how real money boys did it for the sport, not the glory.

Then she realized that those were friends of Jean, which meant he wasn't too far away. As soon as the thought ran through her head, that's when she caught sight of Jean across the room, making it rain. She tried to act as if she didn't notice him, and kept focusing on her Big Spender. The more she blocked Jean out, the more he went from dancer to dancer and out of spite spent crazy money on them. The entire time he threw bread on the other girls, he stared at Calliope, but she would never acknowledge him. Instead she put her all into making Big Spender happy and boy was he hers.

I know good and well you ain't coming up in here with that foolishness on my job. She knew this night was about to go easily from good to crazy in a matter of minutes.

Big Spender was just about out of ones from making it thunderstorm and motioned for the manager to come over there and asked him for ten thousand more ones. As the manager walked away, Jean asked, "You know how much that clown sending for?"

When the manager said with great pride, "Ten thousand," Calliope made sure she looked into Jean's eyes with a smirk, as if, top that.

While waiting for the manager to return with the cash for Big Spender, she still danced; he was good for it. And that was Jean's cue to come over. He started throwing money on Calliope. "Charity." He leaned in."Me and my niggas know ain't no dance for free, so since your benefactor is out of cash, you can be my charity case. I don't have no problem helping the needy," he said with a smile, and then threw a handful of a stack of ones on her.

She picked up that handful and threw them back on him. "Nigga, I don't need your shit. Your money is counterfeit as far as I'm concerned."

"Everything a'ight, baby?" Big Spender asked.

"Stay the fuck out of lovers' quarrels, my man. You don't want none of this."

Big Spender stood up, mildly exposing that he had a pistol on him. That's how Jean and Calliope both knew that Big Spender was somebody with some supernatural clout in there. No one got in with a gun or any kind of weapon and there were usually no exceptions to the rule, for that matter.

"I wasn't talking to you." Big Spender shot a firm look at Jean and didn't flinch. "I was talking to the lady."

Jean was drunk as a skunk but he was still fearless and with an ego the size of the Atlantic Ocean. He wasn't intimidated and he got up in Big Spender's face. "Your contributions here are no longer needed."

"And your presence over here is not wanted, needed, or welcomed. The lady doesn't want your money," Big Spender said with a slight smile.

Calliope saw the fury in Jean's eyes and knew that Big Spender's light remark was weighing heavy and this could go from bad to real ugly in a matter of seconds so she intervened. She got in the middle of them both. "Listen, fellas, we not going to do this."

She put her hand up for Jean to calm down and then she told Big Spender to give her a minute, before she walked a couple of feet away to talk to Jean.

Big Spender nodded. "I'll be right here, baby."

"Why in the hell you bringing this bullshit on my job?" she asked, while the manager was coming in her direction toting the ten thousand ones over to the table where Big Spender was. When she saw him placing the money on the table this domestic dispute with Jean wasn't even important anymore. The only thing she wanted to do was to get that money from Big Spender's hands into hers. She eyed Rabbit; he was the guy who went around the club raking the money up for the girls when they were in puddles of dollar bills.

"I need another minute, and about two more trash bags, Cinnamon," Rabbit alerted her. "Might as well clean up your playground so he can make it thunderstorm." Rabbit's comments added insult to injury.

"I'm not bringing nothing on your job. I'm just enjoying you and myself over there with that lame. Acting like you can't speak and shit. I thought you were jealous because I was dancing with other girls."

Honestly it did hurt her feelings a little but she couldn't dare let him know. "Why would I care?" she asked, then she decided to hit him with a jab. "I have the biggest spender spending his money on me, and me only, while you spreading yours around thin."

She knew that cut Jean deep and he looked like he was about to smack the cowboy shit out of her, but again, Big Spender saved the day. "You ready, baby, cause everything all set over here."

"Motherfucker, do you see me talking? Now you being disrespectful," Jean said with slurred words. "I'm talking to my whore, motherfucker."

Cinnamon had had enough. "Okay, Jean, you need to go." She was pissed and hurt all at the same time. She looked for security and had motioned for them to come over and assist her.

"Oh, you her pimp now?" He nodded. "Let me understand, you a pimp?" Big Spender asked. "Because a few minutes ago, you said it was a lovers' quarrel. And if this is your woman and you pimping her, how does that work, or you her pimp and you in love with your whore? If so, that's not good pimp practices for sure."

Jean tried to swing at Big Spender but was so drunk that he missed. When he did he grabbed the bottle of rosé and when he did security grabbed him and escorted him out of the club.

She was so apologetic to Big Spender and her mood was thrown off. She wanted to cry but she couldn't. Not there, not in front of all of those people and especially not the other dancers. Big Spender tried to comfort her, he told her to sit down and talk to him and take a load off her feet.

"I'm supposed to be entertaining you, and making you feel stress-free, and you are the one who seems to be making my night. It should be the other way around."

"Well, it seems like you need a real friend, and a realer man in your life." He grabbed her hand.

She smiled. "You read my palm correctly."

He looked into her eyes. "It seemed like there is so much more depth to you than meets the eye."

She nodded, showing her dimples. "Yes, there is."

"I'd like to get to know you and maybe we can be friends and I can help you accomplish some of the goals you want."

"That would be nice." There were so many men frequenting the strip club proclaiming to be Captain-Save-a-Ho. And then there was that handful who were really looking to do so. "My superman," she said, and kissed him on the cheek. "Thank you for everything tonight."

"Well hopefully this can be the start-up of many miraculous nights to come." He kissed her on her hand.

They talked for the rest of the night and under the circumstances, she exchanged phone numbers with him and agreed to go to dinner with him the next day. Which was something that she never did. She almost never met men outside of the club, because once she did, then what was the purpose of them coming to see her and spend money. Once they got to know her, she was no longer a fantasy and there was nothing left to their imagination, and that was a gamble that normally she wouldn't take, but this guy was different. He was alluring, charming, and mysterious, and one dinner date may just help.

"Think I'm calling it a night," he said. "You promise as soon as you wake up, you going to call me."

"I promise!" she said with a smile. She gave him a hug. "I can't thank you enough, for everything, and the headaches you got from my ex—and the way you support my hustle, for calming me and comforting me. But most of all for the conversation."

To really make her night, Big Spender gave her half of the ten thousand that had been sitting on the table. "Here, I will give you half of what I got here." He smiled. "I guess this is persuasion to call it a night, huh?"

"Yes it is!" she agreed.

Calliope was floating on cloud nine, heading to the dressing room to get dressed to go home. When she approached her locker, she saw that it was already opened and there was nothing inside of it. Everything had been taken. "Ain't this a bitch?" she screamed. "Who the fuck took my shit?" Everything was gone. Her entire workbag, shoes, cell phone. Everything. Not only her expensive custom costumes but also her sweat suit that she wore to work. She had nothing to change out into. She was outdone.

She told the housemother and she said she would look into it.

She started to tear that locker room up, and turn it upside down but she didn't. The sun had risen, and most of the girls were gone anyway and the morning shift was coming on. She was pissed at the thought that she'd have to go home scantily dressed. Though her neighbors might have suspected, that would be all they needed to confirm.

Someone gave her an old smelly shirt and she slipped that on over her dance clothes but she wondered if she should just settle for her dance clothes.

Thank God that she had valeted her car, or else she wouldn't have her keys or a way home.

Once she stood outside, she saw one of Jean's homeboys walking over to her. He handed her a sweat suit. "Man, that nigga passed out in the car, over there. He was trying to wait for you. But he had too much to drink."

"Thank you." She kindly accepted the clothes.

"You know he love you, he just don't know how to show you."

"So he tricks off and on the girls that work with me and then manages to get my locker broken into?" She laughed with a slight chuckle. She slipped on her clothes and thanked the guy again. Once her car was pulled around, she loaded her money into the car.

She pulled off thinking of how much of a bittersweet night it had been overall. Though her feelings were hurt and emotions were still running wild, she had made in one night what most people made in a year of working.

20

Ring...Ring...

The ringing of the doorbell startled Calliope. She was sleeping like a baby and tried to block it out because she didn't want to wake from her peaceful slumber. Someone was mashing down on the doorbell and the annoying sound wouldn't go away. "Got-damn it," she said, wondering where in the hell was Compton or his girlfriend, Neka, who seemed to be at their house more than hers and more than he was even there. She stumbled out of the bed not wanting to even remove her eye mask that read BEAUTYREST that did an immaculate job at keeping the light out of her eyes so she could sleep during the day. She was afraid if she exposed the light to her eyes that she would not be able to continue her sleep.

RING! Then she heard loud knocks turn into pounding. As much as she hated it, there was no way to stop this ringing noise. She gave in to acting as a blind woman to get to the door.

RING! Still followed by knocking.

When she removed her mask, she grabbed her robe and

headed to the front door. Her first thought was that if it was Jean she was going to really go into psycho-crazy-woman mode. Just then the noise stopped. The visitor must have gotten the message that she wasn't there and if she was, she wasn't answering and decided to leave. Thank God, now she could get more of what her body was yearning for, rest. The second she was back in bed and had pulled the covers back over her head, that's when it got real. The tapping on her bedroom started and then someone started calling her name, "Calliope. Calliope!"

She removed her eye mask and peeped out of the plantation blind. She saw Mocha standing on the other side of the door. "Oh, shit," she said. She jumped up and hurried to the front door to let Mocha in.

"Girl, I thought I was going to have to call Fred, the Fed, and tell him to knock your door down for a dance." She joked of one of her faithful clients.

"Girl, if you knew the kind of night I had, you would have just let me sleep," she said as she went down the hall and into the bathroom to pee. Mocha followed her and stood at the door.

"Girl, I've been calling you all morning, afternoon, and evening."

"Evening?" she questioned, turning her nose up as she was pulling the toilet paper off of the roll. "What time is it?"

"It's almost nine, girl."

"Shit!"

"No shit," Mocha said. "Me and some of everybody been calling you all day."

"Girl, you have no idea what kind of night I had. Shit was

mad real to the point I don't even know where to start. My Big Spender found me at Imagination and Jean came trying to make me jealous, spending on every girl in the club but me. And that shit backfired on him when my Big Spender sent Jiggilo and his people in the vault for me!" She smiled as she washed her hands.

"Girl, I heard. They were talking about that shit all the way over at the Sugar Shack."

Calliope started brushing her teeth, and asked, "For real? Damn, news travel."

"You ain't no gossip traveling faster than the ho stroll girl," Mocha said.

"Did you hear that Jean got some hoes to break in my locker and steal all my outfits, my phone, dancer bag, just everything?"

"That's 'cause he don't feel you should dance and though he don't show it he really love you. You know he feels like his woman shouldn't be dancing at no club."

"Well, if that's love, then I don't want or need his love. He hits me, he doesn't talk to me, he doesn't want me to work and make money, but what is he doing for me, besides getting me fired?"

"Well you know." Mocha started to give her in-depth opinion on the situation but she didn't. She looked at Calliope as a little sister she wanted the best for. "I told you that Jean was crazy and I'm not going there with you but that's not why I drove all the way over here, damn near broke in your house, and probably got the police waiting for me to come out so they can arrest me for breaking and entering," she exaggerated.

Calliope went back and jumped back under her white sheets and white comforter to warm up from the blasting air conditioner. "So what's the scoop, what got you over here?"

"I got a call from the Shack and they said that your Big Spender was looking for me. Girl, I got dressed and went up there thinking that this man about to spend on me, I'm about to take over your sloppy seconds."

"Oh yeah . . ." She was puzzled because she knew she was supposed to call him. She wasn't shocked that he was back over at the Shack, but she was a little disappointed that he didn't waste any time. But that was the typical man that frequented a strip club. This is what they did. Club hopped and chilled with the biggest booty or baddest chick from club to club. "What he spend?" she asked, curious as to how he was moving, trying not to get in her feelings. She just took him to be so different.

"Girl, I get over there and know, I'm going to be able to come up in a big way. As soon as I get there, he only wanted me to get in touch with you for him. He said you weren't answering. I called, no answer. And then I called Compton. He said when he left you were asleep, and that's when I came over. He broke me off to get you to call him. He said he gotta go home to Texas and it's a must to see you before he leaves."

Calliope smiled and that's when Mocha pulled out her phone and called Mr. Big Spender for her and just like that sleep was no longer a priority. Getting to Big Spender was on the top of her list.

21

Calliope and Big Spender's timing wasn't hitting on nothing. By the time she called him, he was already on the way to the airport. She was able to convince him to take a later flight. He would've changed the day altogether but it was a family emergency that required him to be at his mother's bedside for a surgery the next morning. Calliope understood and respected that. Hell, she wished that she had a mother who was worth her dropping everything and running to.

Happy that they were able to squeeze a quick dinner filled with great conversation, at the end of the night he wrote on a small piece of paper a promissory letter, promising her that he'd make it up to her.

She felt that Lou was definitely different from any of the other guys that she had encountered but, hell, she really hadn't taken the time to get to know any of her other customers.

Now she was at work, thinking of Lou, couldn't seem to get him off of her mind. Cinnamon was in her zone and was about to turn it up a few more notches when one of Jiggilo's bouncer goons crowded her space.

"Jiggilo wanna see you," he bluntly said. She sucked her teeth, because what she heard was that he definitely was one person who could sure mess up a wet dream. Jiggilo was the owner of the club and she heard he was narcissistic, sarcastic, egotistical, and he ran that place like it was the army. "In his office," said the bouncer goon. She knew that he most likely wanted to talk to her about the episode from last night about Jean. She was pretty sure that he was going to try to smack her with a big fine, but she was willing to bet that he wasn't going to stress the foolery about her locker getting broken into or her workbag getting stolen.

"Not now." Cinnamon asked, "Can it wait?" Not bothering to hide her instant irritation, she was trying to make money, why wouldn't he wait until after her shift?

Julio, a tall, muscle-bound Spanish Rico Suave–looking guy, whom she was currently dancing for, must've felt her tension, locked eyes with the bouncer goons, and echoed, "It can wait until I'm done, right?"

The two men, Julio and the bouncer goon, were at a Mexican standoff.

The flunky bouncer goon wasn't a sucker at all, and Julio had plenty of heart and could definitely hold his own even a long way from home. Holding up a finger, the bouncer goon said, "One song. On the house." Then using the same pointer, he pointed toward another big-booty dancer standing a few feet away. "Let me introduce you to Toxic."

Toxic, with smooth midnight skin, a banging body, and

pretty face, though not as half pretty as hers, stood with her hands on her hips. In the business it was called a ho stance.

A close second, Toxic was Cinnamon's nearest competition in the club. Cinnamon wasn't a hater by a long shot. And there was no denying Toxic was one lethal bitch, yet Julio hesitated at first, he wanted who he wanted and didn't feel nobody should give him what he wasn't interested in. Cinnamon wasn't mad; she respected loyalty.

Bouncer goon prodded by reminding him, "She's on the house, my man." He gave Toxic the eye and since she had his attention, she spun around in a circle, giving Julio a better gander at the goods.

Papi Chulo was slowly turning into Toxic's Papi Chulo, in front of Cinnamon's very eyes. She fumed, not sure who gave in first: his big head or the little head, threatening to tear the zipper from the seam of his jeans.

Papi Chulo compromised, palms up. "What the hell," he said.

Lust, as it does in most relationships, had TKO'd over loyalty.

"You will come back, right?" he asked Cinnamon, and she nodded.

Stepping into Papi Chulo's space, with a little something extra in the provocative sway of her hips, Toxic rubbed Cinnamon's nose in her small victory.

Though she and Toxic were each other's competition, it was still all love between the two outside of the club. She rolled eyes playfully. "Petty bitch." She smiled, fully understanding that as much as she wished it was, there was no loyalty in the strip club.

They'd gotten no more than a few feet away when Cinnamon stopped cold in her tracks and turned to the bouncer goon.

"Nigga, is you fucking crazy?"

Bouncer goon watched her attitude. He said, "Jiggilo needs you—I get you. End of story. That's it. That's all. Now let's go."

"What let's go? What the hell he want that couldn't wait and warranted to giving a free dance to my client—shit, ain't we trying to make money around here?" she asked.

"Don't matter, Jiggilo's the boss," bouncer goon said, not really caring about her attitude at all.

Cinnamon had been working in clubs, off and on, since she was seventeen years old doing what she had to do to take care of herself and Compton. But when she first started working at the Sugar Shack some years ago, Jiggilo noticed her. Even though he ran the bigger and better clubs, he always seemed to roam into the smaller holes-in-the-wall to see what hidden treasures he could find, and there was no doubt Cinnamon was definitely one of them.

Though he'd never admit it to her face, even as an inexperienced dancer she was always one of Jiggilo's favorites; he loved the way that the manager Mookie from the Sugar Shack always featured her on certain nights, and it never failed, how the high piles of dough rolled in for her. All the bigger and better clubs tried to approach her, but she remained loyal to the Shack.

Jiggilo knew he had something extraordinary on his hands and he had to put insurance on his investment. A year into her working the club, he too couldn't resist her. He so badly wanted to make her his woman.

The Glamorous Life 2: All That Glitters Isn't Gold

Though she was young, she was a long ways from being dumb. She learned a lot from ear hustling in the dressing rooms, while the older dancers poured their hearts out to each other. The dressing room was how she decided what role she would play in the game and what things she wouldn't let play her. It was there she came to the conclusion that her existence in that club was for one reason and one reason only—to provide for her and her brother. Not for the drugs, not for the alcohol, not to marry any of the patrons, not to make friends (though she was glad that she picked up a couple on the way), not for the tri-sexual acts that went on freely in the clubs but for the money and the money only! With that being said, she herself needed insurance just as well.

Two years of him propositioning her, and she would never even take him serious, only becoming his friend and making him one of her allies. But she knew that he wanted her bad so at times she may have taken a little advantage of it. Especially when she needed a job, she called him up and he skipped protocol with her, no audition, no nothing. She just showed up and there was a gig waiting for her.

"He's your boss, not mine," Cinnamon shouted over the music in protest.

"You work at Imagination, don't you?" Bouncer goon gave her that "this is a rhetorical question" voice and a stupid look. "And Jiggilo's your boss then. Just go see what the man wants," he added. "You know how y'all do anyway"—he gave her a dirty smirk—"you know you and the boss man." She hated that the bouncer thought that her and Jiggilo had something going on.

Relenting, Cinnamon made her way through the club to

Jiggilo's office. On the way she spotted her brother and his boys making it rain.

Three years ago, she'd given him five bills to go shopping. He was now not even legal and though he loved his sister, he still had his own thoughts of how things should be done. He was the man of the house and should be taking care of his sister. Instead of buying sneakers and clothes the boy purchased a zone of crack. Partnered up with a friend, and now they had half of his part of town on smash.

Bro, out with a few of his boys enjoying the fruits of their labor, saw her looking at him and he saluted her with two fingers and a lopsided smile.

He funny, she thought to herself, and then shook her attitude because he always seems to put a smile on her face.

Mental note: Tell the bartender to cut back on his drinks. The boy was already tight, never been one to really control his liquor anyway. And he didn't make great decisions when he was drunk. She shook her head, shot him a smile back, and kept it moving to Jiggilo's office.

Outside the office door, Cinnamon took a deep breath, gathering her composure. There was no need to exasperate things by waltzing in the place with a shitty attitude.

She knocked on the metal door.

"It's open." Jiggilo's voice was muffled by the thickness of the security door.

Cinnamon pushed her way inside, the office reeked of endo and cherry incense. Jiggilo sat at his desk with a neat pile of coke in front of him. To Jiggilo's left, sitting in an overstuffed chair tastefully arranged in the corner, was a cat Cinnamon had never met before.

She took one look at him and she knew what time it was with him. His watch was the first thing that stood out. The diamonds were bouncing off the mirrors that laced the walls of the office. His dark chocolate complexion complimented the pink polo-style high-end shirt and white linen fitted slacks he was rocking. The dude was fine as fuck but in a metrosexual sort of way.

Jiggilo made the intros. "Cinnamon meet Peter, Peter meet Cinn." Then he went on to cut to the chase. "It's simple. I need for you to take care of me and my friend, Peter."

Take care of . . . she thought for a second and then tried to keep her composure. *No he didn't go there. I know good and well he didn't go there.*

"Lap dance?"

Jiggilo started laughing. "You know better."

Hands on hips and as much as she tried, she couldn't control it. Some of that stank attitude she'd been suppressing returned. Cinnamon made it clear. "Look, I don't think I'm his type. Nor yours anymore, for that matter." It was obvious Peter and Jiggilo were more than just friends. More like fuck buddies, if not an outright couple.

That was the secret, although there were a few whispers. Nobody really knew for sure but the truth of the matter was that Jiggilo was as gay as a pink French poodle.

An ass bandit . . . a chicken hawk . . . a fudge packer—a straight-up bitch.

In Cinnamon's mind, there wasn't much lower you could

drop on the totem pole than that (cum intended). She had no problem with people being gay, but she had a major issue when men would engage in relations with women and yet men were their preference. And that's exactly what Jiggilo did. He toyed with the dancers in the club using his power and position to make them make fools of themselves. But she knew better and that wasn't her.

One night, she and Mocha were out on a night on the town, hanging out. She had spoken to Jiggilo on the phone earlier that day and he was trying to convince her to come over to his house and spend some "quality time" with him. Like always she'd declined him, but since her and Mocha were lollygagging around town, with a little time to kill, they decided to go around to Jiggilo's house. While Mocha sat in the car talking on the phone Cinnamon found the shock of her life. Some pretty-looking guy much like Peter had about a dozen inches of meat packed up Jiggilo's butt. If there could really be any ass left after being reamed with a thing the size of a small baseball bat, she thought.

"I'm freaky," Cinnamon said. "But not that freaky. You know I don't rock with that. . . ." Her voice trailed off. She wanted to say what she really felt: that he was a disgusting motherfucker, well father-fucka, but chose to stay civil. ". . . Stuff," she finished instead.

Jiggilo hovered over a line of coke from the desktop. "What type of *stuff* is that," he asked, attitude unchecked.

Ignoring the question, Cinnamon said, still remaining calm, "How about I go get Shimmer or Toxic for you? Not only will she be happy to please . . . she's a lot freakier than me, so you two should have bunches of fun together."

Jiggilo snapped, "Bitch, you don't tell me who the fuck *you* gonna send in *my* office. I do the telling around this here bitch."

Since she had caught him in the act, the two of them pretty much stayed out of each other's way, and respected each other's boundaries and were always cordial friends. But recently, since she'd been working at Imagination, she had noticed that he seemed a little reckless, drinking in excess and now the coke.

He got up in her face. "You feel me?"

This nigga bold, huh? Cinnamon wasn't sure if it was the coke making him act a fool, or if he was showing off for his undercover lover. Either way, she didn't flinch an inch.

"Nigga . . ." Cinnamon stared Jiggilo straight in his dilated, coked-up eyes. "I said I don't do that shit. Never have and never will," she spat, and rolled her neck around.

Another sniff of the coke, Jiggilo was flying high.

"Oh—you will," he snared. "Shit is about to change around here anyway. Tired of you walking around here, like *you* own the place and your shit don't stink."

Cinnamon had never prostituted her body to a man nor woman and wouldn't start now. This is what made her so exotic and in demand even after years of dancing. Men always wanted and chased what they couldn't have. If and when she fucked, it was because she wanted to, not for money, and damn sure not because a nigga threatened her.

She pointed to her lips. "Read my mother-fucking lips: I will . . . not!"

Acting like a bully he stood up and in her face. Then Jiggilo offered and ultimatum. "Do what I tell you, or get the fuck out of my club."

"Cool." Her nonchalant response threw him for a loop, temporarily.

"Neko been checking for me to come work at his club anyhow," she added.

That remark pissed Jiggilo off, prompting him to run off a slew of threats. "I'll throw you out the club, I'll see to it you don't work in another spot in Miami."

"Blah, blah, blah," she said over top of his words, not even caring if she pissed him off.

"I'll blackball you," he spit out like he was shooting bullets—as if those words could kill her, and they could definitely murder her career as a dancer.

Strip club owners in Miami were predominately male and a close-knit society for the most part. Blackballing a chick, for any reason, wasn't uncommon since dancers seemed to come a dime a dozen, but usually it was for constantly fighting or forcing the owner to pay fines, but in this case it was just because of personal reasons.

"You would try to do some shiesty-ass trick shit like that, wouldn't ya?" But Cinnamon had her own ace-in-the-hole, Neko. He had another club in the city, not as big as Imagination but the clientele was still star-studded as well, and Neko despised Jiggilo's bitch ass. For that reason alone, he would hire her and welcome her into his establishment with open arms. And the best part about it was Jiggilo knew that she knew.

But he wasn't dropping his bluff. "Try me," he said, "as good as blackballed. You can sell hamburgers, standing up; or fur burgers, on your back, bitch. Make me no never mind. Me being the gentleman that I am, I may even turn you on to a few good johns."

Done with his bullshit, fearless Cinnamon shot back. "Being that you and your sissy over there are the only two people in this room that probably enjoy slurping cum, how about I turn your bitch-ass on to a trim."

Jiggilo pimp-smacked her so hard she heard ringing in her ears.

Tasted blood in her mouth.

As much as they used to argue and go back and forth, he had never hit her before. So she was shocked. From the mirror on the wall behind Jiggilo's desk she saw a small trickle of blood from a busted lip crawl down her chin. She couldn't help but stare at it.

"What the fuck you looking at, you disrespectful bitch?" Jiggilo wasn't finished. "One more chance," he taunted. "You gonna service my *man* or get the fuck out of my club?"

Cinnamon, feigning like she was considering the ultimatum, took a deep breath, coughed up a thick ball of phlegm in the process, and spit a loogie in Jiggilo's face. Bull's-eye.

"Is that a good enough answer for you?" she asked, and before he could shake the shock from the hog spit, she picked up a chair and tossed it into the antique mirror to make her point. "Now suck on that!" Before storming out of his office and heading to the ladies' dressing room, she screamed at the top of her lungs, "Cock sucker!"

———

Back in the ladies' dressing room, bouncer goon stood over her while Cinnamon emptied her locker. "Look, I don't need no babysitter to get my shit outta this raggedy-ass mother-fucker."

"I feel ya, but just doing my job."

"Yeah, doing your job caused this shit," she said, trying to shift the blame to him. She was minding her own business dancing for Papi Chulo and out of the blue he comes disturbing her and taking her down to the office of the bullshit. Now she was out of a job.

He did feel a little bad that it had gotten to this point.

"And where the hell were you when this nigga hit her?" Toxic came to her defense. "Talking about you here to protect us."

Toxic hugged her. "Call me later, but gotta go because now my regular looking for me."

"Girl, what happened?" A few nosey chicks tried to get in her Kool-Aid, but she tuned them out. Put on her Chanel "hater shades" aka "Bitch Blockers" and bounced. The little temporary phone rung and it was Lou, Big Spender, now back in Texas, and she took the call. She told him she'd fill him in and would call him back as soon as she got in the car.

On her way to the door, she bumped into her brother. When he grabbed her hand and asked, "What'd it do sis?" she sucked her teeth under her breath, wishing he hadn't seen her. "How come you leaving so early with all this money in here?"

"What I tell you about coming in here to party anyway?" she snapped back at her brother, like she was his mother, but knowing good and well he'd been hanging out at the strip clubs against her wishes for many years. Besides, he was practically raised in the clubs and was no stranger to that whole strip club life.

"Bam just got out of jail and we celebrating." Then he focused in a little closer, "But what's up wit yo lip?" He looked closer still. "Blood? A busted lip?"

She wiped her face in the dressing room but obviously hadn't done a good job.

Unconsciously, her tongue dotted out, removing the speck of dry blood from the corner of her mouth.

"Don't lie to me, Calliope." Compton never called her Cinnamon ever. It was only her stage name and alter-ego. He would never acknowledge it. To Compton she was and always would be Calliope, his big sister, the woman not only who raised him but to whom he owed everything.

Toxic was walking by and said in Compton's ear, "Jiggilo hit her," and made eye contact with Calliope and kept going.

He couldn't believe his ears, and then he needed confirmation. "Did this fuck boy nigga Jiggilo hit you?"

She couldn't lie to him. Never had and though she knew this would probably be a good day to start, she couldn't do that to her brother. "Yes. Jiggilo hit me," she confided.

A cloud of anger washed over Compton's face. Eyes got dark, darker than she'd ever noticed.

"I'm gonna kill that nigga," Compton said calmly.

She'd expected him to make a scene, hooping and hollering. But the way he'd said what he'd said, Calliope knew her little brother, who wasn't even of age, was dead-ass serious.

"I can't let you do that," she said. "Not tonight. Not like this."

Compton wasn't trying to hear her passivity, even if it was for his own good. "Promise me," she said.

"Okay."

"Okay what?"

"I promise, sis."

"Thank you." She let out a sigh. "I'll see ya later then?"

"Sure," Compton said, "I'll call if I don't come home. Might check on one of my lil' chicks."

Calliope walked away knowing that this chapter of her life was officially over but not knowing that Compton had made his promise to her with his fingers crossed.

22

"*Fuck that!*" *Compton said* out loud once his sister walked away and was out of earshot.

His blood was boiling so hot he could've lit a spliff off his forehead. Compton took a long swig from the green bottle he was holding. The imported, amber-colored beer, although cold going down, did nothing to extinguish the inferno of anger burning in his belly. All he could seem to hear in his head was Big Jack's words about him protecting his sister and how she was all he really had. It was true and there was no questioning or second-guessing what he had to do or the lesson he had to teach or the point he had to make.

The Glock, concealed on the small of his back, felt like it weighed a ton, reminding him of its presence. "What you gonna do?" it seemed to ask. "Barbecue? Or mildew?"

For as far back as Compton could remember Calliope had had his back. When Shelly—the bitch that hadn't earned the right to be called Mom—used to go to town on his hide, simply for looking too much like his deadbeat sperm donor, it was

Calliope who came to his rescue time and time again. Even if it meant getting her butt waxed too.

His sister never bothered a soul or took advantage of anyone at times when opportunities presented themselves to her. As many drunk dudes that went in and out of that club, and were so wasted when she had them in the VIP room, she could've gotten them for all the money in their pocket but she never did. She didn't deserve anybody putting his or her hands on her and Compton wasn't going to tolerate it. If Jiggilo didn't know, he was going to learn tonight.

In front of the metal door that was put in place to fortify Jiggilo's office, Compton stood with his gat in hand. He'd wait all night if he had to for the coward to come out. For some reason, not sure why, he put his hand on the brass knob. And to Compton's surprise and Jiggilo's the knob turned.

"What the fuck you doing?" Jiggilo shouted when the door to his office flew open. Tried to sound like he was in control, but his eyes—especially when he seen the gat—conveyed shock and fear. In the corner, some gay-looking dude wearing a pair of super shiny, white slacks pissed on himself. Seeing the chrome, he knew it was going to be trouble.

Compton told Jiggilo, "You and I have a piece of business to settle." Then he looked to the pink shirt. "Mind your business," he firmly said. "Now sit the fuck down before I lay you down."

Peter plopped his ass down. Jiggilo sucked air into his chest. Compton figured that it was a fusion of drugs Jiggilo had sniffed and the fact that the man had known him for quite some time from afar that brought on the air of arrogance.

Did Jiggilo see a weakness? Compton wondered.

Stepping from around the desk, Jiggilo said, "Put the gun away Compton. We can talk like men if you got a problem, huh? You know you like a son to me."

"You ain't no father to me, nigga. Not even a brother, so don't even come with that."

"Well, I always looked at you as one. Like me, you were raised in these clubs. We can talk like brothers."

"Let's talk then," Compton offered.

Maybe what went down between Jiggilo and Calliope was just a misunderstanding. Calliope could go hard when she wanted to but it didn't matter; the thought of anybody wanting to put his or her hands on his sister to hurt her didn't make any kind of sense to him. His sister's face with the blood popped in his head, prompting him to talk. The heel of the Glock slammed against Jiggilo's temple, splitting it to the white meat. "Do you hear me now, Jiggilo?" Two more cracks upside the dome. "How 'bout now? This is the way *men* talk, Jiggilo. Bitches put their hands on women."

Crack! Crack!

Blood spurted from Jiggilo's face like a faucet. The last blow broke his nose. Jiggilo dropped to his knees and put his hands up to his face. "Okay! Okay! Okay!"

By the way he strained to get the words out Compton figured he'd broken Jiggilo's jaw as well. "You took care of your business, young blood. Let it go." It came out: *ooh ook air uv oar izness, ung bud. Et it 'O.*

The jaw was definitely broke, but Compton wasn't finished.

Click! Clack!

Compton ratcheted the gat, a fresh .40 caliber slug jumped in place.

"You 'fraid to die, Jigg?" he asked him with the tip of the gat in his ear.

Promise me, Compton.

Sometimes . . . promises are made to be broken. Nothing was promised in the streets, that's what made it fair . . . the equality of the unfairness.

Compton wrapped his index finger around the trigger. Like the coward he was, Jiggilo begged for his life. It took eight pounds of pressure on the trigger and he was currently at five pounds.

A little more pressure: six pounds.

What was that smell?

"You shit your draws, Jigg?" Compton asked. "Don't worry, I heard that's what happen when you die anyway. So, no one'll know you let go a few seconds early."

Seven pounds . . . one to go . . .

Promise me, Compton.

Plow!

The only sound after that was Compton's heavy breathing.

Jiggilo, stretched out on the floor, was still alive. He was knocked out from the last blow. He'd hit Jiggilo instead of killing him for a few different reasons. He would've had not only Jiggilo's death under his belt, but he would've had to rock the friend to sleep too. Double homicide wasn't what he needed over his head. Not for nothing Jiggilo did take him and his sister in and Compton appreciated that. And lastly, he'd never broke a promise to his sister . . . crossed fingers or no crossed fingers. But the one promise he'd made to her years ago on that old raggedy porch was that he was going to take care of his sister, and that was one promise he never intended to break.

Pink polo was trying to disappear under the chair, butt all in the air. And just for the hell of it, Compton took a running start, and broke his foot all up in his ass, simply for just being a pussy. Then he laughed because he was a smart guy not wanting any parts of it.

Before he dipped, Compton whispered in Jiggilo's ear, "Next time, all bets are off. You feel me?"

23

4:00 A.M.

From an aluminum thermos, Officer Conners swallowed a sip of his famous home-brewed, premium coffee that his wife always sent him off to work with. He always bragged about the fact that even hours later, it was still hot. The thermos had been a Father's Day present two years ago from his youngest of four daughters. He loved it and the coffee, which always seemed to give him the energy he needed to take on the bad guys.

Senior Officer Theodore Conners was a veteran on the force for decades for the Miami police department. He could've made detective a long time ago, but he simply didn't want it. He didn't need the hassle, paperwork, or the extra hours the job demanded. In six more months Conner would retire to a full pension, God willing, and he just was buying his time.

His partner, Officer Adams, drove the squad car. "Don't know how you drink so much of that stuff," Adams said with a sour face. They'd only been partnered up for a year now, but Conners liked the kid, even though, at twenty-four and still wet behind the ears, Adams could be a little pusher and gung-ho at times.

"Been drinking coffee since I was in the army." He nodded at the can of Red Bull holstered in the cup holder. "They didn't have that shit back then," Conners said.

Adams beamed that cocky smile of his and downed half of the can. This was his eleventh of the night. "Lot of things you guys didn't have back in the day, huh?"

"That's one of the things wrong with you new pups," Conners fired back his own jab, "you all too caught up with computers, smartphones, and energy drinks."

"Is that so . . ." said Adams, piloting the squad car into the Miami Gardens subdivision.

"Yep. I do believe that it's quite so, young pup." Conners, knowing how much Adams hated being called an immature canine, laughed when Adams rolled his eyes.

"Hey." Adams suddenly perked up. "Didn't we get a call on a suspect driving a new model, platinum Range Rover? Big rims?"

"Assault and battery," Conners answered.

"Look up ahead."

Sure enough there was a truck matching the description. The occupant, possibly the suspect, still inside.

Adams, eager to the end the shift with a collar, said, "I think we found it."

After taking another sip of his coffee, Conners made the call. "Light it up."

Going upside of Jiggilo's biscuit with the gat had felt hella good . . . his only regret, not croaking the bitch-ass nigga.

After bashing fuck-boy's face in, Compton dapped his boys for holding him down, in case any of Jiggilo's goons popped up. "Don't mention it," they'd said. His three top dogs. "Calliope's like a sista to us all."

The four left Imagination before anyone was the wiser. Too early to call it a night, Compton hit a few more spots on his own, getting his swag up. Decided to bring the morning in with a drive-by booty call from his girl Melody. She had the body of a goddess combined with a devilish sex game. After he smashed the two, he planned to go home and take his sister out for breakfast.

Breakfast was Calliope's favorite meal. Compton navigated the Range into a parking space. Radio on 99 Jamz, left to turn signal, push the cigarette lighter: a mechanical hum . . . as the hydraulic stash box blossomed from the dash. Compton removed the pistol from the passenger seat and placed it in the secret compartment then closed the box back into its original position.

Next, he killed the engine.

Getting out of the Range, something didn't feel right to him. Like how an antelope must feel in the wild, just before being attacked by a predator lion. Out of his peripheral he spied his predator.

Five-O. Fuck!

Be cool, he thought. Click. Locked the doors to the Range. If the police did get at him, they wouldn't be able to enter the truck without his permission, which they wouldn't get, or a search warrant. Even if Jiggilo's punk ass had pressed charges, an assault beef was candy, as long as the five-o didn't knock him with the cannon or the work he'd be fine.

Woop-Woop!

They flashed the strobes to see how he would react. Then it dawned on him. How could he have been so fucking careless?

Forgot about the zone of hard in his jacket pocket. He was supposed to've hit Black Mike off with the coke at the club, but told him to kick rocks after Mike tried to play him with short paper.

The black-and-white came barreling down the street, V8 engine roaring.

A lion in pursuit of its prey not waiting to be knocked with the work, Compton got in the wind.

Hopped a six-foot wooden fence.

The black-and-white skidded to a stop. That's all the time he needed to toss the coke. But before he could get it out of his pocket, there he was.

Flying over the gate came a young cop, like he was king of the jungle. The coke was stuck on the zipper of his jacket pocket. He tugged harder and his hand came out with the bag. Now all he had to do was lose the wannabe king of the jungle.

Four shots rang out. He was hit. The first one caught him somewhere in the back. Felt like the spine. His legs quit working instantly. Before he collapsed the other three hot balls slammed into various targets on his body. He had no idea where the bullets had struck, because he'd already blacked out.

His last thoughts were: *lion, one, antelope, zero . . . I love you, sis.*

6:48 P.M.

A spectacular orb of fire arose from the eastern horizon. A picturesque view, worthy of a being eternally captured on a postcard. A few hours from now, basking under the brilliance of the sun's rays. Every vacationer's fantasy.

There's that . . . then there's reality. Yellow police tape cordoned the area from curious onlookers. "Where the fuck is it?" Senior Officer Conners was exasperated. "We need to find the gun, Joe."

Thus far the only thing the eight-block search had turned up was a small bag of rock cocaine. Nothing close to the deadly weapon Officer Adams swore he'd seen the suspect brandish before discharging his own service pistol.

Adams swore on everything he loved, "There was a gun. I wouldn't have fired if there hadn't been."

Adams seemed a lot less sure than he'd appeared before they'd canvassed the area. The other officers, Conners could tell by their body language, were ready to call it a day. The only reason most of them hadn't was because they wouldn't have wanted to be hung out to dry if the boot were on the other foot.

Conners listened as his partner went over his version of exactly what had taken place during the pursuit for the twentieth time. It didn't change the fact that no weapon was found, which would substantiate Adams's account of the events.

"The victim of the assault," Adams asked his partner, "said he'd been beaten with a pistol, right?"

Conners gave him a sympathetic look. This wouldn't be the first time, and surely not the last, that an unarmed perpetrator was mistakenly shot. It came with the job. Normally, the incident would go down as just another day in the streets, trying to serve and protect. However, this wasn't the best of times for fuck-ups.

"It don't matter what the guy at the night club says," Conners lamented. Al Sharpton was in town bloviating about a black kid that had gotten shot by a white convenience store owner. This was the type of situation Mr. Sharpton loved to make a spectacle out of. If he sank his teeth into it, he'd not only ask for Adams, but he would be hit with a ridiculous wrongful death suit and the city would have one too many. Maybe Adams would even get time in the joint himself. "You better pray that kid lives," Conners advised in a foreboding tone. "Pray he lives."

24

Franklyn Memorial housed one of the best trauma units in the country. But not even the best surgeons in the world could save every life, every time.

When Calliope rushed through the sliding double doors of the emergency room, she was only concerned with the life of one.

She'd found out her brother was injured by a call that came in the middle of the morning.

"They shot your brother," the voice screamed from the other end of the phone. Panic and despair in the caller's words jotted Calliope from her sleep. "They shot Compton. They shot Compton!" Then hysterical crying.

Praying that this was someone's bad idea of a prank, Calliope asked, "Who is this?" Hoping the person would hang up and say sike but they didn't.

The girl said a name, but Calliope was too startled to process it. The caller's name wasn't important and the call wasn't a prank.

Oh, my God.

Calliope jumped out of bed.

Already getting dressed—jeans, T-shirt, and sneakers—she asked, "Who shot him? Where did it happen? And what hospital?" At least he was still alive.

The caller filled her in best she could. "It's all so crazy," the girl said.

The emergency room was filled with the sick and injured, waiting to be seen—all emergencies weren't created equal. Some people were filling out forms while others tried to convince their friends or loved ones that everything is going to be all right.

Mostly lies.

Calliope hustled to the reception desk, where an overweight white lady with smokers' breath and teeth casually asked, "How may I help you?" The nametag pinned to her lavender smock read Annie.

After Calliope had gotten off the phone with the girl who'd called her—one of her brother's girlfriends—everything had been a blur. She didn't even remember the route she'd driven to the hospital.

She told Annie, "I need to know if my brother is okay."

Annie blew out a pocket of the bad breath, like she had better things to do. "Do your brother have a name?"

Ignoring the attitude the heifer was throwing, Calliope said, "Compton, Compton Conley."

A pause before finger stabbing at the keyboard. Another pause . . . then more stabbing. "Says he's undergoing surgery. Multiple gunshot wounds."

Didn't know he'd been shot more than once. "Is he going to be okay?" she asked.

Annie was on her fifteenth hour of an eighteen-hour shift. "I'm not a doctor," she said. "Just a tired nurse."

If the bitch don't check her, 'tude, she gon' be a beat-down, tired nurse.

"Calliope?" It was the voice from the telephone call she'd gotten earlier. "My name is Neka."

Neka was gorgeous. She had met her before but today seemed to be different when she saw her.

"How'd you recognize me?" Calliope asked, momentarily taking her mind off the nurse.

With a bright smile that her red eyes didn't match, Neka said, "You look just like your brother—well, I mean, he looks like you. Is he going to be okay?"

Calliope cut a murderous look at the derisive nurse. Then gave her attention back to Neka.

"I'm not sure," she said. "All I know is that he's in surgery."

Neka's face contorted as if someone had stabbed her in the heart with a rusty knife.

At that very moment, an athletically built guy with curly blond hair sidled up.

"I'm Doctor Thomas, are you here in regards to Compton Conley?"

Doctor Thomas looked more like a surfer than surgeon, she thought.

"I'm his sister." And all of a sudden, she surely knew that the doctor had bad news.

"You might want to have a seat," Doctor Thomas suggested.

That bad?

25

They got off the elevator on the eleventh floor, one floor above the ICU. They walked down the hall to a semi-private room. A stiff cream-colored curtain used to split the room in half was drawn open. At the moment only one of the two beds was occupied. An aroma of a cleaning agent hit them in the face. Neka's eyes began to tear up once they were fully inside. Calliope wasn't sure if the rudimentary waterworks were from the industrial-strength sanitizer or Compton's unfortunate plight.

Resting in the first bed next to the door, Compton lay hooked to a network of machines and IVs. His eyes were closed, yet the machine above his bed, the function of which was to monitor the contracting and dilating of his heart, peaked in a perfect rhythm. Though her heart had skipped a few beats, she had to thank God he was breathing on his own.

He seemed so peaceful. The doctor had said his condition was touch and go from the beginning, but Compton was a trouper. It would be a while before he got back to normal activities, but the worst part had come and gone. *Thank God.*

Calliope placed a hand on the sheet that rested above her brother's chest. She felt it rise and lower with each breath he took. *Why did he have to be so damn hardheaded?* she thought. Then she smiled at the answer. *We are who we are.*

Calliope started to blame herself. If only she had not left the club that night. If only if she had made him leave with her. What had she been thinking? She knew better. Had she been there, this would have never have happened. She had let her emotions override her intellect, and now these were the consequences. This was all her fault. She searched her mind, wanting to find someone else to blame, but there was no one. Maybe Big John for instilling in them that they had to be each other's keepers, but then again, they had decided that long ago.

"I'm here, me and Neka are both here."

Neka squeezed a tear from her eye and tried her best to sound uplifting. "Hey, baby. I'm right here," she said. "If you need anything." Neka took Compton's hand into hers. It was difficult for Calliope to watch her brother lie motionless in a hospital bed, but she pulled it together and continued to chat with him as if it were all good. Trying to make him feel better, the way she'd always done. For a few seconds the only sound in the room was a soft humming that was coming from the machine. Compton busted the bubble of silence when he opened his eyes.

"He's awake," Neka said excitedly.

"Compton? I'm right here, baby . . ."

Compton's eyes scanning the room smiled when they landed on his sister and girlfriend. It seemed as if the room brightened.

Seeing his face light up was better than winning the lottery for Calliope. Then suddenly his hand twitched.

"You okay, Comp?"

More twitching. The twitching turned into jerking.

Neka in the beginning stages of panic, turned to Calliope. "What's wrong with him?"

Calliope had no idea. The twitching had changed into violent spasms; his arms were flailing wildly. His body seemed as if it wanted to hop off the bed.

"Help! Help! Help!" Calliope screamed for assistance. "Nurse! Doctor! Someone get in here!" Frantically she pushed the emergency button, over and over. . . . When help didn't arrive quickly enough, Neka flew out of the room to see what was taking so long. "You are going to be fine," Calliope said to Compton. She hoped and prayed it was true. Compton continued to shake and spasm as if he were having a seizure.

Whatever was wrong with him—it was getting worse.

Finally, a doctor stormed into the room, followed by a team of nurses. "Get back," the doctor said to her as he took charge of the situation. Next, the doctor started barking orders at the nurses. One nurse filled a syringe with a clear liquid while another put some kind of cream on the paddles of a defibrillator. The doctor tore the gown away from Compton's chest, allowing the space for the defibrillator to connect with the skin.

The nurse shouted, "Clear!" And then they jolted him with an electrical shock. Compton's body jumped from the bed before falling back in place. The spasms had ceased but there was only faint activity from the reader monitoring his heart.

"Again!" The doctor ordered.

They repeated the process in tandem. The other jammed the needle into Compton's arm, while her colleague greased the defibrillator paddle for a third run.

The doctor, noticing for the first time that Calliope was still in the room, shouted, "Get her outta here!"

A nurse tried to escort Calliope out of the room. "Get your hands off of me," Calliope shouted at the nurse. "I'm staying." She was firm and the nurse knew it. The nurse glanced at the doctor, the doctor continued to work frantically, trying to save Compton's life.

"Clear!"

Zap! Nothing.

Nothing the doctor did worked. Nothing made the flat line on the machine pulsate again. Then the doctor dropped his shoulders and turned to Calliope. "I'm sorry. . . ."

Nooooo! She screamed at the top of her lungs. This wasn't happening. She broke down crying, and the tears would not stop. At that moment, she felt like she had lost everything. What did she possibly have left to lose or to live for?

26

Jean paid for the funeral; and no expense was too great for his heavy pockets. In fact, Jean thrived off the recklessly extravagant purchases he made in order to put Compton away like a top-tier baller.

All of the guests were encouraged to wear white, and the custom-built casket was designed from a cocaine-white Lexus that was identical to the one that Calliope pushed, except hers was convertible.

When Calliope had asked, why a Lexus, of all the models of whips he could've used, Jean said, "That decision was easy." He looked directly into her eyes. "Compton always talked about how you rolled for him. So in his final resting place, I wanted him to feel like he was riding eternally with you."

The lavishness didn't stop with the casket. The rented out Club Ice, another renowned strip club, and placed Compton on the center stage.

Distraught beyond incomprehension, Calliope sat in the front row and watched baller after baller pay their respects to her little brother. Many of the men she had never seen before, besides a few from the club, but after viewing her brother's body, all of them gifted her with envelopes stuffed with various amounts of money. Calliope was nobody's fool and certainly not naive. She knew that it was really Jean that they were showing homage to, but the garish display of love and wealth, however feigned, was touching.

A plethora of white orchards and white roses hung from every perch in the club. Most of the men drank Cognac, some from bejeweled pimp cups, while women sipped premium champagne from crystal flutes. Everything about this gathering was boss.

A live performance by Scarface made heads nod, and evoked more than a few tears but nothing could have prepared Calliope for what took place midway through the proceeding. Dressed in a tight black dress, a late arrival sidled down the aisle to the front row, seemingly distressed. The woman sat next to Calliope and made a show of dabbing her eyes with a silk handkerchief. *Unfucking believable.*

Calliope hadn't laid eyes on the woman who had given birth to her for more than seven years until now. "What're *you* doing here?" Calliope asked the question like a pile of shit would've been more welcomed.

Another live performance took the stage, this time it was Plies.

As if everything between them were tickety-boo, Shelly said, "Why would you ask me such a question?" Peering at the Lexus that held Compton's remains, she said, "That's my baby. Almost fifteen hours of labor."

This bitch is crazy, Calliope thought. Shelly had given up the rights to being a mother a long time ago. Out of curiosity, Calliope asked, "Where have you been?"

Shelly perked up, already forgetting that she was supposed to be in mourning. "At first, I moved to Orlando. Then back to New Orleans, needed to get my shit together."

That was probably where Shelly was still chasing these men folks around. Calliope knew the answer; still, she asked, "Did you find 'em?"

The question blindsided Shelly. "Find who? I damn sure ain't find God, if that's what you are talking about." Calliope almost laughed in Shelly's face and contemplated spitting in it.

"Let's cut the bull, Shelly. We both know you left me and Compton behind, so you could run behind some nigga you hoped would take care of you. We saw you. When those child protective people had us in the backseat of the car, we saw you standing in the crowd with the neighbors, looking at us being hauled away."

Shelly was speechless for a second. "What was I supposed to do?"

"My question is, did you find him worth it? Was living the life of a trifling bitch worth abandoning your seed?"

A moment passed. The tension was so thick that a Revlon relaxer couldn't straighten them out. Jean, sitting on the other side of Calliope next to Moo-Moo, asked, "Are you okay, baby?"

Calliope told him that she was fine.

Finally, Shelly said, "Don't act that way." And then she tried to give some lame excuse on why she would have stayed in Miami.

It fell on deaf ears. "I don't want to hear that shit, really I don't, Shelly. This ain't the time or the place."

"You will never understand."

"Fuck you!"

"I'm telling the truth, begging to be forgiven. If it wasn't for that I would've never left."

Someone passed Shelly a drink. She emptied the flute in one tilt and then she took another flute and repeated that, and then asked for another one. The champagne went to her head and loosened her up so much, she had the gall to ask Calliope to introduce her to a baller.

"Do your mother a solid."

The bitch had some nerve but keeping it real Calliope felt kind of sorry for Shelly. The woman was still in search of something that she'd never have: love. "I'm going to keep it twenty-four carat with you, Shelly." And her mother was all ears. The catch in this place looked like they were worth a mint. If Shelly couldn't find love, the dollars would do as a fine substitute.

Calliope gazed into her mother's avaricious eyes and said, "I would introduce you to all the shit you could eat. Just go somewhere and die."

A rejected and dejected Shelly dropped her head, with the dollar signs in her head falling to the floor.

27

Sixty seconds...

Every time the skinny hand of his Rolex swept around its diamond-encrusted face, he figured, at least a hundred Gs exchanged hands in this spot.

The problem.

The exchange wasn't rocking out in his favor today. He'd already dropped forty stacks, and (another glance at his Presidential Roley and a forty from his wife) it was 6:32.

Damn.

He'd placed his first bet less than twenty minutes ago and hadn't a thing moved but the money. The good thing . . . Well, it was hard to find anything positive out of dumping car money in what seemed like a bottomless pit in the time it took to take a shower, but at least the evening was still young and in the blink of an eye things *could* change . . . for the better.

All he needed to do was to not run out of money before he ran out of bad luck. Luck . . . yeah, right, seemed to not to be able to find him in this setting.

Over the hum of slot machines, dice tripping over one another, moans of sorrow (from losing bettors), and woops of excitement (from winners), a melodic voice, which was owned by a long-legged waitress, offered him a drink, a watered-down vodka and cranberry. "Thanks."

The drink pusher only smiled and gracefully skated away in a pair of four-inch heels, and what seemed like a skater's gold-sequined miniskirt. Her job was to get the gamblers intoxicated, so they peel paper to the dealers, tables, and slots—not to socialize.

The name of the casino was Magic City. Lynx wondered if the waitress moonlighted at the strip club that bore the same name. He'd been there once. Then he thought: Magic City was a fucked up name for a casino. Tragic City was more befitting. He was beating himself up for not trying his luck at the Hard Rock Casino when the dealer, a short, balding dude with tiny hands, asked if he wanted a hit.

He glanced at his card in his hand and shook his head. What he needed was for Lady Luck to drop her hot, charming ass "like it was hot" and give him a lap dance until he got his paper back up. But until then, he was on his own. It was just him and the cards.

"Hit?" Either the dealer thought that he was hard of hearing or just moving too slow, because he repeated himself.

Lynx responded by tapping the felt table, twice, near his hand.

Fingering the shoe, the dealer removed the next card. Not the bent-over, brown loafers he wore, but the contraption to his left that the casinos used to hold and dispense the playing cards. In the time it took for the dealer to put in play the card he'd plucked from the box, barely a second, Lynx's heart accelerated a half beat.

Ten of diamonds.

The dealer started to ask whether Lynx wanted another hit, but the amalgamation of frustration and melancholy telegraphed upon Lynx's face preempted the query. In one smooth, practiced maneuver, the box man relieved him of his discarded hand and the two thousand-dollar black chips he'd wagered on it.

A distant voice, from somewhere off in the casino, called, "Jack Pot!" while Lynx manipulated one of his last remaining eight chips, end-over-end, between the knuckles of his left hand. When he was losing, the exercise of dexterity helped him to relax.

The chip: seemingly floating from the top of his fist, to the bottom, back to the top . . .

Lynx had to admit, if even just to himself and no one else, eight grand was a lot of bread. Maybe he should quit, for now. Try his luck again at another time. Another day. Another casino . . . But tucking his tail wasn't what he'd come to Miami to do. Contrary to the white lie he'd told his wife, Bambi—"This is strictly a business trip, baby"—before leaving her and their toddler daughter in Virginia, he'd flown to Miami for one reason . . . and one reason only: to gamble.

He reminded himself: scared money don't win money.

Besides . . .

His present thoughts eluded him and for the first time that night, his eyes left the cards.

The distraction came in the form of a young lady posted up across the casino floor, about fifteen or so yards away. Painted-on jeans, fitted, jade, silk button-down blouse, short hair (Halle Berry short not Grace Jones short). Her skin tone was the color of baked cinnamon. But it was her eyes that quickly captured Lynx's attention.

They seemed to be homed in on a . . . target. Lynx tried but couldn't make out the object of her rapt attention. Then, as if she felt his stare, she turned her head toward him. The look lingered, although not for long, but long enough to deliver a faint smile and leave an impression.

An invitation?

Most gamblers, if not all of them, are at least a little bit superstitious, and Lynx wasn't of the exception. Luck—good or bad—can be contrived from any thing, place, or person.

"Hit? Hit? Hit?" When the dealer offered him a respectful shit-or-get-off-the-pot glare, the floating chip froze between Lynx's pinky and ring finger. He added it to the other seven, and then bet a stack.

Like it had been scripted, an ace of clubs slid from the shoe, followed by the queen of spades.

Blackjack.

"Yes," he said to himself, and the adrenaline started to flow through his bloodstream.

Lady Luck may not have given him the lap dance he'd wished for, not yet, but as Lynx banked that she'd smile on him, she did.

He bet the sixteen Gs all on the next hand.

And won again, and again.

He zeroed in on the spot where his good luck charm had been standing—good, she was still there. Blackjack after blackjack, winning hand after winning hand, he looked up again and tried to focus on the target before she escaped Lynx's line of vision. This time, to his dismay, she didn't invite him into her eyes. But Lynx sensed that she felt his presence all the same.

Three more bets, everything on the line with each wager, and his charm didn't disappoint. His stake had swelled to $158 thousand. He'd attracted a few onlookers, encouraging him to push the envelope. Bet it all one more time. The innate urge to do it, risk it all, double or nothing, was tempting.

However, for some reason Lynx thought of a scene from *American Gangster*. Where the Asian dude tried to tell Frank Lucas that it wasn't the same as quitting when you stopped while ahead. Unlike Frank, Lynx heeded the sage advice.

Chips in hand, it was time to formally meet the woman that'd fueled his change of fortune. His Dame of Fortune.

But when he looked up, she wasn't there.

So now what? So . . . go find her, he thought.

Good luck with that.

Lynx strolled around the casino looking for his mystery woman. Where she had disappeared to, he didn't have the foggiest idea. Right when he was about to chalk it up as a loss, there was she was sitting at the bar. He headed over to the bar and when he got closer it seemed that she had a blank, empty look on her face. Before fully approaching her, he noticed that she was preoccupied, with all her attention focused on something or someone. Who? He couldn't pinpoint it right away.

"You mind?" he asked, taking a seat anyway on the empty bar stool beside her.

"You might mind," she said, never looking up from her drink.

"How could I mind sitting beside such a beautiful woman such as yourself?"

"Look, it's just this simple," she said. "I'm not the one you need to be sitting near, and damn sure not talking to you. And no, I don't want your drink."

"Damn, you don't want my drink?"

"Nope, or your conversation. So spare me the pleasantries."

"May I ask why?"

"Busy."

"Exactly what got you so busy that you won't have a drink with such a handsome guy."

"Look, didn't I tell you that I'm not the lady you wanna be seen with, playboy?" Calliope said to him.

"Whoa," Lynx said, followed by a jolly laugh. "Far from being a playboy." Then he instructed the bartender to get another drink.

"So you all say that," she commented. Then she looked up for the first time at him, and his eyes met hers. He noticed that she looked as though she had been crying, and her eyes were the window to her soul. It was apparent that she had something heavy that she was carrying.

"Now look, it's like this. Now maybe if we were in a different place in a different time, I might give you some conversation. In fact, I'm usually good at carrying on a conversation. But I got something real heavy on my plate that I gotta deal with. And thanks for the drink, but shit is about to get real funky in a few minutes, so if you not trying to get caught in the middle of some shit you have nothing to do with, then please keep it moving."

Lynx couldn't help himself, he had to know. "What in the world could make such a beautiful woman want to do something so ugly?" He put his hand on her cheekbone. "Nothing is worth you losing your freedom for."

"Listen playboy, you don't know my plight, or my story, so I'd appreciate it if you keep your preconceptions to yourself." She had tears in her eyes still.

"You are right, I don't know your story but I got time. I got all night to listen." He pulled his chair a little closer.

"What? Some guy broke your heart?"

"Yup. In more words than I could ever share and the pain . . . unspeakable." Which he saw in her eyes.

Lynx was silent for a minute. "The hurt you feel, baby. Trust me, the next man will come along and mend. After all, time heals all wounds."

"No man could ever heal the pain of my little brother, who I raised as my very own son. We were left to fend for ourselves, and we were all each other had . . . all I had." The thoughts of Compton, and her admitting aloud that he was gone, made the tears come.

Lynx handed her a napkin and he made her comfortable enough to share her story and her plans for what she was going to do to Jiggilo in the middle of the casino. Lynx was not only a great listener, but he took it all in and began to assess the situation for her.

"Listen baby, my heart goes out to you and that motherfucker what you thinking about plus more and he's going to get it. But straight up . . . right now. It's the wrong place, wrong time. You don't want to spend the rest of your life in prison because of one bad decision. Do you?"

See, what Calliope didn't know was that Lynx was a certified street nigga and knew the ins and outs of the streets.

"So, I'm just suppose to let this motherfucker get away with hurting my family, my own family at that? He's having fun, laughing, balling with not a second thought of my brother. As philosophical as you sound, you know that shit doesn't even sound right to you."

"I didn't say that now, did I?" He flashed her a charismatic smile, took a sip of his drink, and instructed her to do the same. And when she did, he let out a sinister snicker, which piqued her interest. He was a few years older than Jean, which was already six years older than she was. She liked his swagger and his sarcasm, and he was cute. She couldn't wait to hear what he had to say.

"But what you need to understand is that's not the type of thing that you do on somebody else's time. Trust me when I tell you baby. I got the hot buried pistol to prove it."

She sat there mesmerized by his knowledge and his whole being. With his words he finally was able to get a slight smile out of her.

"So listen, so I'm going to tell you what. . . . I'm going to show you the best way to handle your situation."

She raised an eyebrow.

He put up a finger, "but in return, I want you to allow me to repay my debt to you."

She looked confused, and inquired, "What debt?"

"I was way down on my luck until I laid eyes on you. The minute I made eye contact with you, was the second that my luck changed and I'd like to take you shopping and buy you something nice, and have dinner with you. Can we do that?"

Her whole attitude and demeanor was in a different mode. "Sure."

The vibe they shared for the night was magnetic unlike anything that either of them had shared. Was it because when they first laid eyes on each other, the chips were down for them both?

After dinner and the shopping spree, they landed for a drink in Lynx's suite. The nightcap led her to encounter her second sex partner but first one-night stand, which turned into the ultimate sexcapade. Her pent-up anger turned to deep-rooted passion that she never knew existed, which resulted in them making a baby.

28

Three Years Later

The rowdy crowds began to congregate at the first wink of sunrise. Black-and-white squad cars cruised the streets of downtown in an effort to control the elevated enthusiasm, at least to a manageable degree, while keeping a vigilant eye out for "unusual" criminal activity.

Unusual criminal activity . . .

Baltimore is, and always has been, not only known for its delicious crab cakes and its working-class people, but also for its high-crime rates and rampant drug trade. For as long as its dwellers care to even remember, the number of mortalities caused by heroin overdoses has taken a backseat to nothing other than flat-out murder, a corpse at the wrong end of a smoking gun, which, when all said and done, was more often than not drug related as well.

For most people, however, their hardships were suppressed, at least for a few hours, when their beloved Ravens suited up for battle on Sundays on their home turf of the M&T Bank Stadium. The fans come out and show love to the home team whether they are dressed in the team's mascot costume or player's jerseys, are face-painted, or are draped in purple and black pearls. They come in costume to represent their home team.

"I got it taken care of," Lynx shouted into the phone. "Yeah—no problem." He had to cover his other ear to hear the caller over the raucous noise inside the stadium. "Yeah, I know. Things are looking up." His attempt to block out a lot of the noise was futile. He still couldn't hear so he wrapped up the call. "Gotta go." Honestly he needed to get back to the game.

Lynx was relieved to have gotten his hands on a pair of decent seats on the fifty-yard line, midway up. High enough to view all the action without the aid of binoculars but low enough to avoid the nosebleeds. He was able to kill two birds with one stone, see the game, and spend a little quality time with his baby girl, Nya, his seven-year-old daughter. He had been so caught up ripping and running and juggling he hadn't been spending as much time as he'd liked to with his little princess. So, today was their day.

Nya tugged on her father's arm, trying to get his attention. Her long purple-ribboned pigtails rested almost past the middle of her back. Her little face was painted Raven purple and black with a little glitter mixed in, and she was wearing a #52 Ray Lewis jersey with rhinestones around the number, looking like an official, die-hard mini-fan.

"I'm hungry, Daddy."

The second quarter was nearly over.

"Hold tight. We'll get a couple of hot dogs at halftime. Okay, princess?"

Hot dogs and chicken nuggets were her favorite food and her mother never let her have those things, so a big smile covered her face, knowing that her father was going to let her indulge. "Okay, Daddy." But after sitting, she sat still for about three more minutes, then asked, "How long before halftime get here?"

Lynx explained that there were only a few more seconds in the second quarter. "Four," he said, "to be exact," motioning her to look at the clock.

A boisterous white guy sitting on the other side of Lynx, smelling as if he'd just finished swimming in a pool of Jack Daniels, naked from the waist up, pat him on the back and said, "Helluva game, huh?" Before Lynx could utter, "It sure is," the inebriated exhibitionist let out an earsplitting, "*Wheeeew!*"

Nya got impatient tapping on Lynx's arm. She said, "Four seconds is up, Daddy."

Sometimes the girl was too smart for her own good, Lynx thought. "There's four seconds left on the clock," he explained, "but right now there's a time-out, baby girl."

"How long for the time-out?" she asked with a look on her face Lynx thought meant that she was trying to process whether or not he was telling the truth. Like her mother, Nya wasn't easy to BS.

Just when he was about to explain that time-outs lasted anywhere from thirty seconds to three minutes, the two teams took the field, saving him the trouble of his daughter's cross-examination. "This is the last play before halftime," he said instead.

"I want cheese on my hot dog."

"Okay, baby." He nodded.

"And chili fries too, Daddy," she huffed, since it was that easy the first time to get him to agree.

"Mommy doesn't let you have cheese," Lynx reminded her, never taking his eyes off the field for a second.

Before she could rebut, the referee blew the whistle, ending the play and the half.

"No worries, princess, it's whatever you want. You know Daddy always gives you all the desires of your heart," Lynx said as they got up from their seats en route to the nearest food concession. "Let's go." Lynx was in a good mood. The fifty Gs he'd bet on the Ravens to win straight up was a sure thing. Baltimore hadn't given up a game at home in two years, a perfect 15-0 during that time. The streak went back to December 2010.

A sure thing...

After the third quarter, two cheese hot dogs—one with jalapeños—and a Styrofoam tray topped with chili and cheese fries, both teams had paid a visit to the end zone a grand total of once, which meant the Ravens still held on a seven-point lead. The half-naked drunk to Lynx's right shouted obscenities at the Steelers' players every time they made a decent play, his voice drowned out by more than fifty thousand other screaming fans.

Fifteen more minutes, Lynx mumbled to himself. "I just need for you to hold the fort down another fifteen minutes."

"Who you talking to, Daddy?" Nya's eyes beamed to him. "Mama say when you talk to yourself, people may mistake you for crazy or stupid, if you keep talking to yourself and I don't want people to think you are, Daddy."

Lynx snatched a quick glance at his daughter before turning

back to the game. "Don't worry, people aren't going to think your daddy is stupid—I'm just superstitious. There's a perfect explanation for all this, my dear, sweet princess," he said, rubbing her face. "I was talking to the football gods, not to myself."

Nya was quiet for a moment. "I thought there was only one God? And I don't think he plays football," she reasoned. "Besides, Daddy, I don't think there are TVs in heaven, so he can't watch either."

"Best believe," Lynx admonished, "he watches. This—I'm sure of."

Not willing to debate with her father, Nya just sat in her seat trying to put it all together for herself. Satisfied that she was right, she got her phone out and started playing a game.

In the fourth, the Ravens' offense was god-awful.

"Yo, Joe Flacco, stop playing like a high school kid," Lynx said out loud as if the quarterback could really hear him. Luckily, the Steelers weren't playing much better, scoring only a field goal themselves. The Ravens were up by four with less than six minutes to go.

As much as Lynx hated to even think it, he could feel the momentum of the game changing in the Steelers' favor. Baltimore hadn't yet imposed their will. And in not doing so, the Steelers, even playing with their third-string quarterback, believed they could pull off a win. And Lynx was no longer sure that they couldn't. His "sure thing" was beginning to look really suspect.

A couple of minutes later the inevitable happened: a forty-two-yard touchdown grab by Shaun Suisham. The play sucked the air, and life, slam out of the entire stadium, including Lynx. He was too outdone and wanted to kick himself in the ass.

The score put the Steelers up 24-20. Everyone looked at the person beside them, incredulously with an I-can't-fucking-believe-this expression etched onto elongated and stunned faces.

Believe it.

When the clock hit zero, Lynx sat and looked at it for a minute as if somehow more time was going to miraculously appear on the clock. But it didn't work that way. The game was over, and, like clockwork, the fans rushed the exits as if they were trying to escape a bad dream. Tailgaters mourned the loss in the parking lot. Anyone crazy enough to think that football was "just another game" didn't get it. From New York to California and Minnesota to Texas, fans ate, slept, and defecated for their respective teams. Marriages were ruined over the game of football, and if his wife found out about the fifty grand he'd just lost, not to mention the other paper, his may be ruined. Or she may just kill him.

Lynx was slowly shaking his head in utter bewilderment when his phone rang. He didn't need to look at the caller ID to know who was calling. It was the people he'd just lost another fifty Gs to, the same people that he was now into for $165,000.

He released the grip on Nya's hand to face the music on the end of the phone.

Nya stood by her father, rubbing her stomach. "Daddy, my stomach hurt."

"Mine too, baby girl, mine too," he repeated to his daughter as he put the phone up to his ear. "Hello?"

"Daddy . . . I . . . think, I might have ate too much." Nya stood beside her father rubbing her stomach.

". . . Yeah, I know what the numbers are. . . . You're gonna get your paper"— with a lump in his throat, he reiterated— "all of it."

"Daddy, I . . ." Since he was still talking on the phone she swallowed her words. She knew her manners and she exercised them by trying to politely wait for him to finish his call.

From behind her someone bumped her. When Nya turned to see who'd pushed her an ocean of bodies washed past. An old white lady, trying to push past her, and said, "Excuse me, darling," then kept on shoving her way through the crowd and pushed her even farther away from her daddy.

No longer able to see him, Nya tried calling out to him. "Daddy!" She was bumped again. "Daddy!"

She couldn't see him anymore, and boy was she scared. The poor child was too short to see over the crowd; the crowd was too thick to see through.

Again, she screamed: "Daddy!"

He grabbed her hand. "I gotcha," a man said.

That wasn't her daddy's voice. Nya looked up at the face of the man holding her hand. It was painted purple, like hers. "Who're you?" She tried to snatch her hand away, but he was holding on to it too tight.

"I'm going to help you find your daddy," he said, leading her away from the crowd. She tried to lock her knees together, then her legs and feet fell to the concrete, hoping she'd be super-glued to the concrete so she couldn't move, but the man was too strong for her.

Bambi, Nya's mother, had told her never to go anywhere with someone she didn't know, and not to talk to them either.

"I don't know you," Nya said, trying to wrench her hand away from his grip. "Let go of me."

He tried to convince her that he was a friend of the family, but Nya didn't believe him. Strangers told lies.

"I'm going to fall out on the ground and scream if you don't let me go." She'd learned that at school and she was about to follow up on her promise when the stranger said he wanted to show her something that he'd gotten from her mother. The mention of her mother got Nya's attention.

"You don't know my mother," she accused. "Stranger danger," she screamed, but nobody paid attention, so she yelled at the top of her lungs, "Stranger danger!"

"Sure I do. She told me to give you this."

It was a silk scarf, a red one.

"That's not my mother's . . ."

The stranger pressed the red scarf against her nose. It was wet with something that smelled sweet. Then, suddenly, she fell asleep.

The chloroform would keep her out for at least an hour. The stranger picked up what looked to be his very sleepy daughter into his arms. The makeup on both of their faces helped with the charade and, just in case anyone did get suspicious, it concealed his true identity.

29

"*Nyy-aaah!*"

Lynx yelled out his daughter's name again and again and again, spinning in circles in search of her. "*Fuck!*" He didn't see her anywhere. He'd only taken his eyes off Nya for just a split second to answer the phone, and just that quick, she was gone. Vanished.

"Nyy-aaah!"

People started to stare. *Who you talking to, Daddy? Mama say when you talk to yourself, people may mistake you for crazy or stupid. I don't want people to think you are.*

Nya's voice continued to echo in his head as Lynx randomly stopped a man wearing a #20 Ed Reed jersey.

"Excuse me, my man? But have you seen a little girl, about this tall?" Lynx held his hand waist-high. "Long, black pigtails and raven-colored ribbons in her hair? Face painted purple?"

Lynx noticed that the man's face was painted purple also.

And so were the three young boys' that were with him. Hell. Half the damn stadium had painted their faces for the game.

The man seemed empathetic to Lynx's situation, or maybe the look that Lynx saw in his eyes was just sympathy, one parent feeling sorry for another's misfortune. Whatever the emotion that he may have felt, the man shook his head.

"Can't say that I have," he said, and dropped his head. "Sorry."

There was no time to be sorry. A lot of other folks were going to be sorry.

Lynx quickly moved on to the next closest person, then the next . . . and the next . . . and the next . . . With each person he asked, Lynx became more desperate. And more frantic with every "no." He began to run into the nearest ladies' restroom like a mad man screaming Nya's name

Lynx startled a lady who was on her way out. "Did you see a little girl in the there?"

The woman shook her head, and he strode past her.

"Nyyaaahhh," he desperately called out, praying that she was in one of the stalls.

Women shot him nasty stares, fused with a few choice obscenities. A two-hundred-pound, trigger-happy blond chick dug into her purse for a can of mace, but slowed her roll when she saw the I-got-no-problem-with-putting-a-foot-up-your-ass look on his face.

Luckily, he made it in and out of the restroom without anyone getting hurt. After roughly forty-five minutes of fervent searching Lynx found himself inside a police precinct. Primarily used to detain finger smiths (pickpockets) and other types of thieves, bush-whackers (perpetrators of assault and muggers), and junkies (illegal pharmacists), the in-house precinct was built on one of the sub-levels. A policeman behind a desk was unceremoniously pushing papers while chowing down on a roast beef and pickle sandwich. The name tag pinned to his uniform read OFFICER MCELROY. "What can I do you for?" said Officer McElroy with a mouthful of the stinking processed sandwich meat.

It hurt to say it. The five words burned the lining of Lynx's stomach en route to his mouth. "I can't find my daughter." *The shit didn't even sound right,* Lynx thought. *You're supposed to lose keys, maybe your cell phone, but not your child. Never your child.*

Officer McElroy said, "Pretty nice trick you managed to pull off there. I wish I had that problem with my wife." The man couldn't have been more callous if he tried.

Surely the cop didn't understand what he was saying or maybe Lynx wasn't clear on the way he was conveying what he was trying to say.

He still had not digested the words that had just come out of his mouth when he had to cough those same words up again. "My daughter is missing. I can't find her." And the words tasted bitter coming out the second time.

"How long has she been missing—your daughter?"

At this point, the police in general and Lynx had a long history of not seeing eye to eye, and this comedian in blue wasn't doing much to change that.

Lynx took a deep breath to keep from snapping. His going off on the man wasn't going to help the situation any. He looked at his watch. "It's been nearly an hour now. Maybe a little less."

"And where was the last place you saw her?" McElroy asked.

Lynx explained to the officer how Nya was right by his side when they were leaving the stadium—on entry level—when he took his eyes off her for a second to answer the phone.

Derisively, Officer McElroy mumbled, "I see. The phone, huh? I don't even know why you people carry those things around glued to your ears. What did you do before?"

You people. Lynx thought about straightening this lazy, sandwich-eating moron. Lynx was about to respond when the simple cop got to the issue at hand.

"Did you try paging her over the PA system?"

Lynx had gotten a lady from the information kiosk to page Nya three times. After no luck, she was the one who had suggested Lynx try the precinct.

"Yes, I have," Lynx said.

"And?"

And.

"The fuck do you mean? *And.* If I'd found her I wouldn't be here. I've looked everywhere," Lynx said, getting more upset than he already was. "I want an APB put out on her. I want people looking for her. What's the name of that shit they do for those white kids that go missing?" He snapped his fingers with the answer to his own question. "Amber Alert. I want a fucking Amber Alert issued."

Unmoved by Lynx's situation, or his demands, Officer McElroy said, "I understand your anxiety; however, I do know how to perform my F-ing job."

Praying for the strength and discipline to keep from wrapping his hands around this asshole's neck, Lynx held his tongue and kept his hands deep in his pockets.

"Now let's try this again," Officer McElroy continued, "I'm gonna need a description: Age? Height? Weight? And the clothes she was wearing when you last saw her?"

Lynx gave McElroy what he'd asked for, glad to be finally getting somewhere.

McElroy keyed the necessary information into a computer that sat on his desk. "Do you have a recent picture?"

"Sure." Lynx got one from his wallet. It was of Bambi and Nya at Nya's cousin's birthday party. He handed it to the officer. "Will this do?"

In the photo Nya and Bambi were dressed alike in yellow dresses and big floppy hats.

"Pretty girl you got here," said McElroy, smiling at the picture.

"Thank you."

His eyes still on the photo, McElroy cracked, "Yeah, your daughter is cute too." Then he laughed like the shit was too funny.

It happened real quickly.

Lynx shut McElroy up by slamming his fist down his throat hard enough to loosen a couple of his teeth. Immediately the jokes came to a screeching halt. *Should've whipped his ass.* Lynx thought about the jokes while pounding McElroy a few more times for good measure. Two other policemen rushed in from the back room when they heard the commotion. Too bad for McElroy they didn't show up quicker.

"What the hell—" one of them shouted.

McElroy's partners in blue wasted no time breaking up the lopsided fight, giving Lynx a few well-placed wallops with their nightsticks in the process.

30

A black SUV sporting tinted windows hugged the middle lane of I-495, heading north. The driver of the SUV went by the name Big Jack for obvious reasons: he was six four and a cheeseburger short of weighing 275 pounds. His partner Mo rode shotgun.

Mo turned to Big Jack. "You sho she ain't dead?"

Big Jack put a Rick Ross CD in the deck. He wasn't a big fan of the artist as a person (the fact that dude was a correctional officer before becoming a gangsta rapper was hard to overlook), but he liked the music the guy put out.

Once Big Jack found the track, he said, "She's still breathing, ain't it?" as if Mo had asked a stupid question.

"That shit can kill a person that small, if you use too much," Mo said in defense. "She ain't no good to a nigga dead," he pointed out.

Big Jack would have preferred not to have used the strong anesthetic at all, but he had no reason not to believe the girl when she told him that she would fall on the ground and scream if he didn't let go of her hand. That would have been no good.

Mo looked in the backseat.

Nya was still unconscious. A black scarf around her eyes, just in case she woke up before they reached their destination. But like Big Jack said, she was still breathing. Mo could see her little chest moving.

31

"*Yooooo*," *he called out* nonstop, Lynx demanded his one phone call. "I have a right to call my attorney," he said. "This is against my constitutional right."

Finally, an officer wheeled a portable jack down the hallway and parked it outside of Lynx's cell. "You got ten minutes."

The contraption looked like a pay phone welded to a skateboard. The metal cord attached to the receiver was about half the length of his arm. So short he would have to squat down and lean against the bars for it to reach his ear.

Lynx assumed the necessary position and instead of calling his lawyer, he dialed his wife, Bambi.

"Hello."

"Bambi."

"Lynx?" There was a pause before she asked, "Who phone are you on?" Before he could explain, she asked, "How far are y'all from home?"

This was going to be more difficult than he thought it would be. And he thought it would be god-awful.

He said, "I need for you to sit down. Are you sitting?"

"What's going on, Lynx? Just spit it out." He was sure that she probably thought the call was about him being late again. It seemed like this was what the majority of his calls were about nowadays.

He paused for a second, then said, "I'm still in Baltimore. . . ."

"You know it's a school night," she shot back, wanting Nya to get her proper rest and not be cranky in the morning or unproductive at school.

He took in a deep breath, and started filling her in. After giving Bambi the quick version of the situation (yet no less painful), she screamed, "What do you mean, missing?"

Her voice vibrated through the earpiece, bouncing off the three walls of the monkey cage he was in.

"I know you're upset," he said. "But listen to me. I need for you to stay calm. We're going to find her."

"You know I'm upset? Lynx, I'm way past upset. My fucking daughter has disappeared. You lost our daughter at a damn football game. How could you lose our child and then turn around and get yourself locked up? Who's looking for her?"

She stopped to take a breath. Lynx used the opportunity to promise, "I'm going to find her. The police are doing their thing, and the minute I'm outta here, I'm back on the streets searching high and low."

Bambi wasn't satisfied with his plan of action. "I'm on my way there now," she said.

Lynx could hear the anguish cutting through her vocal cords. Over and over and over, he butt his head against the cold steel bars. Bambi was one of the strongest women he knew. But the right blow had knocked heavyweight champions on their backs for the count.

"No," he said. "It's best if you stay home. Nya might try to call you. Imagine how she may feel if she did, and couldn't reach you?"

Bambi was thinking about Lynx's suggestion when the officer that had brought the phone returned. "Time up."

Lynx put his finger up, gesturing for one more minute, but the line went dead.

"Bitch!" Lynx threw the phone down. "Fuck you hang up for?"

"Wasn't me. The phone is on the ten-minute timer. It hangs up on its own, tried to tell you."

Not appeased, Lynx questioned, "How long before I get a bond? So I can get the fuck outta here."

32

It was somewhere north of midnight and the lower-middle-class neighborhood was as quiet as a sleeping baby with a full tummy and a soft mattress. Besides the porch lights that lined the manicured yards along the U-shaped street, the other light was the full moon shining down.

There was a night-light still on inside the yellow, two-story home on the edge of the cul-de-sac.

"Mommy, where is Daddy?" a cute, bright-eyed little three-year-old with jet-black curly hair asked his mother.

"I don't know, baby. I think he's still working," Calliope told her inquisitive son. The truth, she had the foggiest idea where her baby's father really was. "Now come on out of the window and get ready to go back to bed."

"But he said he'd be here to tuck me in," Junior told his mother, his little face twisted into a defiant pout. The sight of him was too cute, warmed her heart.

Calliope hugged her son. "I know, baby. But I think he might have gotten a little caught up at work."

After a few more hugs, which probably comforted her more than it did him, and a warm glass of milk, Junior was ready to go back to sleep.

"Mommy, I want to sleep with you."

One look into his half-closed eyes and she couldn't say no. Calliope knew that her son liked sleeping in her room so he could lie on the side of the bed closest to that window. That way he could sneak and peek out at the cars' headlights going past the house, hoping and praying that they belonged to his father. The fact of the matter was that the boy loved the ground that his father walked on and whatever the man said was law.

To the little con artist, she said, "If you promise to lie down and close your eyes." Then she pulled the covers back on her queen-sized bed so he could climb under them.

"I promise," Junior said with a smirk so big that his mother knew that he was telling a huge fib.

"You have to get your sleep and be rested for day care in the morning," she told him as she tucked him in.

"I don't want to go to that day care anymore." His defiant face popped up again.

A kiss on the forehead. "You always say that until I get you there," she said.

"I just want to stay with you, Mommy." He was stubborn, just like his father.

"You should be with other children, and play games with them."

"But I play games and have a whole lotta fun with you, Mommy."

"Junior, I know what you are doing, and you better start playing the go-to-sleep game."

He just closed his eyes tight, thinking he was fooling her, but he wasn't.

"If your daddy comes, I promise, I will wake you up," she whispered.

"Why isn't he home, Mommy?" he asked again, trying to fight sleep, but slumber was getting the best of him.

She didn't know what else to say, so the lie rolled off Calliope's tongue, like a bedtime story: "He's working, baby." Then she lay down beside her son and put her arms around him until he fell off to sleep. But the truth of the matter was, she wanted and wished that she could say to him, *although I love him to death, your daddy ain't shit,* and frankly she was getting tired of him acting like her house was a revolving door, walking in and out of her life and house whenever he pleased. But she didn't want to be responsible for turning the boy against his father. When it happened, it wouldn't be on her account.

Convincing her son that his father must have gotten tied up and would get there when he could—and finally getting him to sleep—was mentally exhausting. She thought that after all that she would be able to fall off to sleep immediately, but she couldn't put her finger on it—there was something definitely keeping her up. She looked at her son, who was sound asleep on the other side of the bed. She contemplated taking him to his room, but then decided that since he was sleeping so peacefully, by no means did she want him to wake up. So she'd let him stay right where he was, even *if* his jive-ass daddy decided to show up.

For the life of Calliope, she couldn't understand, as tired as she was, why in the world she could not get a wink of sleep. She damn sure wasn't losing any Zs over her baby's daddy. She knew the type of bullshit the man was knee-deep in when she first got involved with him. She should have listened to her head instead of her heart and her coochie. She was attracted to his honesty, she guessed, the fact that he never lied to her about his circumstances no matter how crazy they were. In a strange funny kind of way this seemed to have turned her on. And the fact that he was just so handsome filled with swagger and always showed her a good time even while schooling her to lessons of the game called life.

Calliope was wet behind the ears about a lot but had a great understanding about everything.

Tired of tossing and turning she got up, careful not to wake Junior. It was hard enough to get her son to sleep—since he went to sleep disappointed that his father had not come by to spend time with him or tuck him into the bed like he had promised him earlier that day when the two FaceTimed—that she didn't want to keep moving around in the bed and wake him up. She wished things were different. Well, something had to give.

She finally had both feet on the floor and then she heard something.

What was that noise? she wondered. It sounded like someone was on the steps. Her baby daddy had a key but he always called first even if he was right outside, but it was late still. She peeped out of the window to see if his car was outside and it wasn't. *Hmmm,* she wondered.

Afraid to admit that she was afraid, Calliope cautiously peeped out of the bedroom door to see who it was. Her heart almost jumped out her chest when she saw a man, not her baby's daddy, holding a gun in his hand. *Shit,* she said under her breath.

The home invader wore all black that matched the gun in his hand. She had no idea what the man wanted but she knew he didn't come there to have tea and sing "Kumbaya." She had to think quick to find a way to get her son and herself out of the house and out of harm's way.

Her first thought was to get her son and take him out the back door, but she thought again. The home invader may not have come alone, his partner could be watching the back door. All she knew at that very moment was that she had to act quickly. She gently shook her son. "Junior, Junior," she quietly said to him in a whisper. No soon as he opened his eyes up, she put her finger up to his lips, motioning him to be quiet, by zipping his lips.

"Daddy's"— he tried to utter, but she shushed him before he could get it out and by the look on her face, he knew better than to say anything. She continued to try to analyze the situation. She could hear the intruder in her son's room, searching for what she had no idea.

"Listen, be very quiet. There are some bad guys in the other room, and I think they may be here to hurt us. So I will need you to be very quiet and we're going to activate our super-powers, okay."

Junior nodded.

More footsteps; there were two of them. When she heard

them headed down the hall to the guest bedroom, she knew that after they left the guest quarters then they would be coming to her bedroom. That's when she grabbed her son's hand and made a quick but quiet run for the basement.

Now what? She thought about hiding behind the hot-water tank when she heard the door open. "The basement," one of the men said. She picked up Junior in her arms and quickly scurried across the floor. Luckily, the basement was filled with junk, so that they could not see her as she shoved her son down the crawl space and then proceeded to squeeze herself into the small space behind him.

"Come out wherever you are," the man called out. "There's no way out."

She heard the footsteps coming down the stairs before she saw them. Seconds after, through the louvers of the small door on the crawl space, the black Nike boots appeared and started searching the basement. When there was no sign of them, he was pissed. "Where the fuck this bitch at, man?" The owner of the Nike boots got frustrated and kicked the box of Christmas decorations that Calliope had been meaning to put up on the shelf, almost startling Junior. Calliope quickly put her hand over his mouth so he wouldn't let out a peep. "Hang in there, baby. We're going to be okay."

She just continued to watch, hoping and praying that the intruders wouldn't find them.

"You got them?" Another voice called down from the top of the steps.

"Naw"—the one wearing the Nike boots sucked his teeth— "they ain't here." He sounded disappointed.

"Where the fuck could they have gone?" Deep-voice demanded to know from upstairs.

"I saw her when she turned out the light in the bedroom." He shook his head feeling like he had failed at his task. "They gotta be in this house some damn where."

"Well, we looked, they ain't here." Nike boots headed up the stairs and when he got halfway to the top, he stopped and said, "We'll just have to go with plan B then."

Calliope exhaled a deep heavy breath when she heard the basement door shut. She removed her hands off of Junior's mouth but not before telling him to keep quiet, then, "Not a word, baby."

Who were they? she thought. *And what the hell was plan B?*

Obviously, plan A wasn't to steal her valuables. For a second she tried to think what she should do. How long should they stay put. She waited a few minutes before she slowly, cautiously removed the door to the space they had cramped into and scooted out. "Stay here," she told her son.

"No, Mommy. Don't leave me." He was scared and shaking.

"I need to make sure that the bad guys are gone, so that they don't hurt us."

"I can protect us," he said, pointing to the superhero on his pajamas.

"I know, baby." She kissed him on the forehead. "But stay here for now."

Once she was out of the tight crawl space, she could hear them doing a second tour around the upstairs.

She tipped to the top of the basement steps to evaluate the situation better. The door to the basement was ajar. Good. The latch had been broken for a while, and she'd been meaning to get it fixed.

"Oh! My! God!" she said to herself in shock.

At the top of the steps, she could smell the strong, distinct odor of gas.

Her heart dropped. Plan B was to set the house on fire.

She motioned with her hands for Junior to come over.

Through the cracked door she could see her purse on the counter next to the back door that led to the garage. She was about to make a run for it when she heard the front door of the house slam and that's when she saw flames. Minutes later she smelled the smoke. Where there's smoke, there's always fire. She grabbed Junior's little hand and raced for the bar chair where her purse sat and then ran for the garage door. The key to the car was in her purse. She shoved the key in the ignition, while saying, "Buckle up, baby," and trying to help him with her free hand.

"Lord have mercy," she said out loud, as she hit the garage door opener that rested on top of the sun visor. "Hold on, baby," she said to Junior. Before the door was fully ajar, she took a deep breath, put her foot on the accelerator, and backed the Mercedes SUV out of the garage, barely missing the top of the door. In reverse she pulled out of the small driveway like the devil himself was after her, not giving a damn who or what was in her path.

From on top of the hill up the street Calliope watched her house go up in flames. She tried calling Junior's father, to tell him of the bizarre chain of events that had happened in the wee hours of the night, but the call kept going to voice mail. She must have called him a hundred times and there wasn't any answer.

For the life of her she didn't understand why he hadn't called and wasn't answering any of her calls. He should've known she would have never called him so many times unless something was very wrong, and it was.

With her phone, she snapped pictures of her house, as the roaring fire engines began to speed to the scene, sirens blaring. She sent the pictures to him and that didn't even make him return the call.

She left her baby's daddy message after message. No return call. What was she to do? They didn't have anywhere to go. She didn't have a support system. After all, she had relocated to Virginia when she was pregnant and had been there with him since. The more she called and got the voice mail the angrier she got. She'd never blown up his phone before, so he should've known that something was wrong. The more he didn't respond, the madder she got.

"This shit is fucking ridiculous," she yelled into the phone. "I've called you a million times and still no answer. You can't be serious right now?

"Listen, we moved here for you and you know we don't have nobody else. And if we never needed you before we need you now. Where the fuck are you? We're homeless and you're nowhere to be found." Then, she had a lightbulb moment. "You know what motherfucker? I know where to find your ass."

She put the Mercedes in gear and started driving.

"Mommy, where we going?"

"To your daddy."

33

The forty-five was pointed toward the front of Nya's head. There was no doubt that fear gripped every muscle of her young, seven-year-old body, while tears cascaded from her innocent, doe-like eyes.

"Puh-lease . . ." she begged and pleaded with the man holding her at gunpoint. "Please don't hurt me. I didn't do anything. Please," she wailed in tears.

The iron-beast-looking man before Nya's eyes, waving the pistol, was enormously huge. Easily towering over the average full-grown man, juxtaposed to Nya he looked like a nefarious giant from a dark fairly tale. Unmoved by Nya's crying and pleads, the ogre casually glanced at his plastic Timex. "Time's up," he said to himself in a matter-of-fact tone. He'd waited too long as it was. Then, with as much emotion as a person changing the channel from a rerun of a tired, played-out sitcom, he squeezed the trigger twice.

"Nooooooo!"

The blood-curdling scream startled Ruby awake. "What's wrong, Bambi?"

Still asleep, Bambi's breathing was labored, sucking air like she was in the last leg of the Boston Marathon. Ruby grabbed a hold of her arm, shaking her. "Wake up, girl. Wake up!"

Bambi yanked her eyes open. Her body was drenched with perspiration. Her head swiveled from side to side trying to take in her surroundings like a video camera on a tripod.

She and Ruby had dozed off on the couch, she remembered. So it all had been a dream—Nya getting shot.

"Oh, my goodness!" She looked her over and saw she was drenched. "Girl, you sweating like a pig at the slaughterhouse," Ruby said, trying to lighten the mood. But regardless of how hard Ruby tried to carry the weight and be the strong one, Bambi knew that she was just as worried. It showed in her face, this the first time that Ruby didn't and couldn't put on her poker face. Emotions of sadness, despair, and hurt were written all over her face.

After a few seconds Bambi regained control of her breathing. Inhale. Exhale. "I just had a nightmare," she said to Ruby, who was wishing that this was all only a dream. But the realness of the matter was, it wasn't. So all she could do was pray that it was no more than that and wished like hell that that wasn't mother's intuition kicking in or a sign of the worst to come. She wasn't overly superstitious, well a little, but she still knew that nightmares, like regular dreams, were sometimes mere premonitions of the future.

Ruby needed air herself, so she went into the kitchen. She

took a few minutes to try to meditate to focus hard on trying not to let her mind run wild and think of all the things they could be doing to her sweet little princess. Nya was like the daughter she never had. She loved that little girl as if she were her own, but she wasn't. She was Bambi's child that no one thought she would ever be able to have, and Bambi loved her with all her heart. At that moment, she took a deep breath and reminded herself that she had to be strong for Bambi. She headed back into the room and handed Bambi a glass of water.

"Drink this," she told Bambi.

So caught up in her own cogitation Bambi hadn't noticed when Ruby had gotten up from the couch.

"Thanks, Rue." She took a full, much needed, thirsty sip and it did the trick. The Cîroc she'd drunk the night before must have left her dehydrated, more than she realized. After another swallow from the water glass, she checked her phone for messages. No one had called. Not the police. Not Lynx. No one. Not knowing what else to do, she said, "I think I'm going to go to my bedroom and check e-mails. If nothing else, to give me something to do before I go plum crazy."

Anything to help keep it together, Ruby thought.

Ruby wasn't very computer literate. Her main choice of communication were the telephone, land line—her preference—and snail mail. She was old school like that, felt like someone was always listening and watching. So she preferred to stick with what she knew. But she encouraged her friend to do whatever was needed to relax, even if only momentarily. "You go do that. I'll tidy up in the kitchen, while you swim the Web."

Normally Bambi would've corrected Ruby ("surf the Web," not "swim"), but her mind was so frayed tonight that the unorthodox phraseology *swam* by unnoticed.

Thirty minutes later the doorbell chimed.

"I'll get it," Ruby yelled out to Bambi, wondering who it could be so early in the wee hours of the morning. But nevertheless, she wiped her hands dry on a dish towel, moved about the kitchen to the tall, top, mahogany cabinet, and got the stepstool, stood on it, and opened the mahogany cabinet door. She moved a couple of big mixing bowls around until she found what she needed. Got the .45 caliber out of it, tucked it in the pocket of her card-boarded starched-creased Lee jeans, and headed to the door. As she got a step closer, she hoped it wasn't one of the kidnappers trying to bring static to the house, but if it was, she was definitely prepared to bust a cap in their ass if she had to.

Ruby cut the porch light on, trying to get a glimpse at who it was, totally oblivious to what was about to be revealed.

Disengaging the dead bolt, Ruby swung open the door to two sets of eyes staring at her. Eyes or faces she'd never seen before. One pair were perfectly spaced on the face of a twenty-something-year-old butterfly with smooth cinnamon skin and straight white teeth; the other pair were owned by a little caterpillar of the cutest little boy. Ruby couldn't put her finger on it at that moment, but there was something about the little caterpillar that looked very familiar to her. She decided that whatever it was about him, she wasn't going to let it drive her crazy. She had bigger things on her mind.

Offering a warm smile, which was something she rarely did for strangers, Ruby said, "May I help you?"

But seeing the little mannish snaggle-toothed boy standing there in his little Superman pj's shed a little light on the situation.

"We looking for my daddy," the caterpillar blurted out in a squeaky voice.

There was no denying the child was adorable, but Ruby had no answers for the boy's request. Hell, wasn't we all, she wanted to say. She knew she hadn't seen hers in God knows when.

Before she could say so, the butterfly took over. "Excuse me, Junior, let grown people talk, please, sir," she said, and giving him a look to shush him then let her eyes meet Ruby's. "My apologies, he's just a little excited and sleepy at the same time not to mention been through more than any little boy or adult for that matter should have to deal with in one night or life, period."

"Join the damn club," Ruby said in a dry tone. And then thought that it was after three in the morning. They both should've been somewhere asleep.

"My name is Calliope," the butterfly said.

Ruby gave her a second once-over leaning in the doorway, wondering, *what the hell this woman want? Shit she must wanna use the phone, car broke down and she need to call her husband or something. Thought I was the only one in this day and time who didn't have a cell phone.*

The girl had the skin tone of a fashion model, eyes of an angel, and a voice that sounded like a musical instrument. The butterfly, or whatever name she went by, seemed like she could be harmless, but Ruby was an OG. She knew better, that most of the time these were the types that always ended up being a big stack of trouble.

"Ahem." Ruby cleared her throat before stealing a peek down the hall, toward Bambi's bedroom. Though she didn't feel that they were in any way connected to the kidnappers or that they came to bring any harm, for some odd reason she still had a bad feeling about these two.

"Nice to meet you," Ruby said, and then tried to think of the girl's name but it couldn't come to her for the life of her.

"Calliope," the butterfly said, filling in the empty space.

"But exactly what is it that you want?" Ruby finished. *If this chick needed more than to use the telephone, God help her. Her timing was bad, this wasn't the time or the place for us to be helping no strangers.*

"I'm looking for my baby's daddy," Calliope bluntly said.

"Well, I don't know what to tell you, honey," Ruby said sarcastically. "Shit it's a whole lot of people looking for him, and honey, I truly don't recommend you going door to door in this neighborhood. Chile, these white folks around here will have you locked up for trespassing."

Ruby wasn't trying to be funny at the least. She thought she was giving the poor woman with her bastard child by her side some truly good advice, under the circumstances of the turmoil going on under their roof. The point of the butterfly's visit and the words that she was trying to convey had gone totally over

Ruby's head. Ruby never suspected that Lynx was cheating or carrying on relations with other women. She had always thought of Lynx as an overall great guy and he always took care of home. He was a wonderful husband who loved and respected Bambi. He always gave Bambi all the desires of her heart, love, support for her business, jewels, furs, cars, big house, vacation, and his time. And when it surfaced that she couldn't have any children, Lynx went and made a way for them to adopt Nya as a newborn. The second Nya arrived into their life he was an excellent father and good husband. He was an overall great guy in her book even though Ruby wasn't too trusting when it came to anybody, especially not men.

Ruby's ex Uno had taken her to hell and back. In the eighties she had it going on. Nice house in a middle-class neighborhood, BMW in her driveway, good job with benefits that she could get all the overtime she wanted, the latest designer fashions, and a man who was getting a lot of money but loved her. The two were genuinely happy. They were living high off the hog, until one day the police showed up wanting her to turn state's evidence on Uno and his drug empire. When she refused to, they threw her in jail and gave her the same charges that they gave her man.

Since she wasn't directly involved in any illegal activities whatsoever and had the best lawyer money could buy, she was certain that the charges would eventually go away and she'd be able to go back to living her life. That was very realistic until Uno realized that he'd be getting an asshole full of time. Before the dust settled he had helped himself to a get-out-of-jail-free card, and told on everybody he knew anything on and when that wasn't enough he immediately put everything on Ruby, resulting in her giving ten years of her life to the State of Virginia.

After giving ten years of her life away, she had time to reflect on every lowlife man and she'd seen her share of scoundrels in her day and could spot one a mile away, but for some reason she would have never suspected this type of thing from Lynx.

She'd always known one if she'd crossed paths with one and with all her heart and soul, Lynx wasn't one, but, hey, everyone had one time to be wrong.

It was indeed three in the morning and it may have been the wrong time. But Calliope knew good and well that she was at the right place. She had driven past the house at least a thousand times before and had seen more than hundreds of pictures of Bambi, and had done her research in and out about everything about her baby's father's life and his wife. She knew this wasn't the wife but the wife's right hand. Though she had played it out a million times before in her head, she never thought that it would happen like this.

Bluntly, "No, he lives here."

"Oh, no he don't live here," Ruby quickly said in a matter-of-fact way.

But that was a tap on the arm compared to the next haymaker she cut loose. "His name is Lynx and doesn't Lynx and Bambi live here? This is their place of residence, right?"

Boom! *Wow!* Calliope saw the look on Ruby's face.

The look on Ruby's face was priceless and it read, what the fuck!?! But her thoughts were, *God, please don't let Bambi kill this young lady this morning.*

"Look, chile," Ruby said leaning in closer.

"It's Calliope," she clearly stated her name, stood up straight, and held her own.

"My mama name is Calliope," Junior said, and then his mother shot him a look that silenced him.

Ruby glared at her, like her mother would and gave her a cold stare. "Listen, today isn't really the day for this. Not being funny, but real talk. We got some real serious stuff going on in our world and today ain't the day for the Maury Povich 'you are or are not the father' type bullshit. So."

Calliope put her hand up, and lowered her voice, not wanting to prompt drama or make a scene. After all, they did live in a high-class area. "Look, believe me," Calliope interrupted Ruby, wanting to take control of the conversation because she knew she was dead wrong showing up on these folks' door step in the wee hours of the morning. "If I'd had any other alternative at all, I would've never come here"

Ruby stood in the door seal. "I'm listening." She crossed her arms with a so serious look on her face, trying to talk herself out of pulling her pistol out and telling the girl to get the hell off of her friend's porch.

"Look, I'm not looking for trouble."

"Shit I can't tell. Coming to somebody's house in the wee hours in the morning, seems like you begging for trouble to me."

"Trust me I've had my fair share of it in my day and that's why I try to fly under the radar. But trouble seemed to have found me." She took a deep breath, then started back up before Ruby could say a word. "A little while ago, two men unlawfully came into my house, burned my house down to the ground.

And I think that they wanted to take my baby." The butterfly stole a quick glance at her caterpillar as if she wanted to make sure that her son was still there, like someone could have actually snatched the kid while she was holding on to his hand.

Wow, now that was a doozy, Ruby thought to herself. Still standing there with her arms crossed and popping her gum loudly. *Oh boy, the butterfly is Lynx's sidepiece and the kid is his son. Now this is some real Jerry Springer shit here.*

"Lord help us," she finally budged, but at least Ruby knew why the little caterpillar looked so familiar, now that she looked closer, the boy had Lynx's nose and devilish grin that formed his little mouth. The features were cuter on Junior. Ruby slowly moved to open the door wider. She was dumbfounded at that moment. She gripped her pistol to make sure it was still there in case this girl tried something when she invited the mother and son duo to cross the threshold of her baby daddy's wife's home.

"Honestly, like I told you, this isn't a real good time, 'cause things are a little crazy," as Ruby led them into the den. "But sit in here for a minute, I'll be right back."

Once inside Junior spotted a photo of Lynx in a silver frame on the end of the table next to the sofa, and took off like a bottle rocket. "It's daddy. It's daddy. Look, Mommy," he said with such excitement. He clumsily pulled the picture from its place on the table.

Calliope the butterfly looked on with a sheepish, unapologetic half smile, but not one ounce of shame on her beautiful face.

Oh, boy. Bambi already had more than enough to swallow on her plate without this . . .

As Ruby slowly made her way down the hall, she kept trying to think of the words that she would say to Bambi explaining the visitors who she just invited into Bambi's home. Then for the second time tonight, Ruby heard Bambi belt out a curdling scream.

34

Totally in a state of shock, Bambi screamed at the top of her lungs, prompting Ruby to come running. Her old-school princess-style Reeboks drummed against the hardwood flooring as she hightailed it down the hallway. Ruby busted into the room with her hand gripping the pistol on her side.

"What is it?" she gasped, rushing through Bambi's bedroom door not knowing what to expect.

Bambi shook her head in dismay, her tongue temporarily stunned into silence with her eyes filled with tears. Things had gone from bad to catastrophic in a matter of seconds. One minute she'd been dumping old e-mails from her in-box, reading new postings, trying to keep her mind busy from thinking the worst of where her daughter was, and the next, her heart was trying to jailbreak its way out of her chest by way of jackhammer. She had never felt pain so intense that she thought she was having a heart attack. Still unable to locate her voice, she opted to point to the computer screen.

Ruby peered over Bambi's shoulder at what had rocked her to the core.

Both stared openmouthed at the heart-wrenching e-mail, not wanting to believe what their eyes were witnessing.

Finally, a mortified Bambi managed to croak out the words, "They got my baby." She wasn't the type that could be called a weak person, but seeing Nya tied up like a rodeo calf broke her down. Even though it was obviously the effect the kidnappers were trying to provoke, it was working.

If they'd violated her in a sexual way . . . thinking about it was too much to bear right now for either of them to let their thoughts run wild.

IF YOU EVER WANT TO SEE YOUR DAUGHTER ALIVE, FOLLOW THESE INSTRUCTIONS.

Nothing about this madness is simple.

1. IF YOU CALL THE POLICE—SHE'S DEAD
2. I WANT 500K
3. I'LL NOTIFY YOU IN 48 HOURS W/ FURTHER INSTRUCTIONS OF WHERE TO DROP BREAD OFF

A JPEG file attached to the e-mail contained the horrible picture of Nya, wrists and ankles bound by a nylon-looking rope. Bambi zeroed in on her daughter's eyes and she was terrified and scared shitless. Bambi at that moment felt useless and like she wished that she could change places with her daughter but it didn't work like that. All she could think about was where was she supposed to get money like that from. Her lavish party-planning business wasn't the thriving business it was five years ago. She still had steady clientele and events to put on, but the reality of it was, the country was in a depression and people didn't have money like they used to. Everybody seemed to be cutting back on everything, and that included events. Now they were still partying but just on a lower scale, and she was thankful for that, even though they expected her to stretch a dollar as long as she could.

She knew that she needed to get the money, and quick.

"Where am I suppose to get a half million dollars from, Ruby? I got a little more than a hundred thousand and in our joint account is a whole other story, but besides that . . ." Her words trailed off.

Blood coated the surface of Ruby's bottom lip, she was biting down on it so hard. "Where there's a will, there's a way," she said.

Ruby wasn't just talking out of her ass to make Bambi feel better. Ruby genuinely loved Nya with all her heart and would do whatever she had to do to assist in getting the baby girl back.

Bambi snapped out of her zone when she heard a patter of footsteps racing down the hallway, causing Bambi to look up. At first, she thought she'd imagined the sound. Up until a little boy with familiar features teetered into her room.

Bambi looked up and thought she was seeing double. She

shook her head, to make sure her eyes were not lying to her or her mind playing tricks on her. There in front of her stood a mini Lynx.

The two made eye contact. "Hello, where is my daddy?" Junior asked Bambi.

35

Sergeant Johnson kept it real funky for a jake. It turned out that this wasn't the first time Officer McElroy had acted in a manner other than professional; this was one of the reasons he'd been assigned to the desk, and not on the street. Instead of slapping Lynx with assault and battery on a officer—a charge that would've netted him a parole violation and a few years off the blade—Sergeant Johnson went with the much less severe misdemeanor charge, which (if found guilty) only carried a maximum of twelve months, no violation.

In total Lynx spent a little more than twelve hours locked down. His lawyer would eventually get the whole thing dropped.

He was straightening out his clothes when Sergeant Johnson passed Lynx a large manila envelope. "Your personals."

The envelope contained Lynx's wallet, cell phone, and car keys. "What about my daughter?" he asked, pocketing his things. "What's being done about her?"

Sergeant Johnson's expression was somber. "We put out the Amber Alert." He didn't really sound all too optimistic about it. "And all of our mobile units have her description," he said. "For now, that's all we can do."

Lynx took his stuff, exited the cell, and made his way out of the jail to the streets to try to figure out his next move.

Lynx quickly made it to his car and began cruising the streets of Baltimore as if he was going to find his daughter just strolling down the block or something.

They all look guilty, Lynx thought of the characters he passed as he drove aimlessly through the ratchet streets of B'more: the three saggy pants, young street pharmacists trying to push mediocre dog food to the smack heads. The cat with the dreads down to his back, selling CDs and incense in front of the McDonald's. The chick rocking too much makeup, white jeans, thigh-high faux leather boots, dodging through traffic like a bumper was attached to her ass. Even the gray-haired lady sitting behind the wheel of the Honda next to him at the stoplight seemed as if she had something to hide. Everyone was guilty of at least one misdeed or another, Lynx thought. Most of which were none of his business.

The only crime committed in Baltimore that Lynx gave a damn about was the kidnapping of Nya. He wondered just how many people he may have passed were in on i—

Honk! Honk! Honk!

"I see the fuckin' light." Lynx tapped the gas just hard enough to make the high-performance Audi boogie thru the intersection, quickly eating up nearly two blocks' worth of asphalt, before veering last minute into the parking lot of the

Quick Mart/gas station, a good spot to tap off both the tank and his stomach.

But first thing first, he thought. Instead of pulling up at the pump, Lynx guided the Audi into one of the three self-service car-wash bays, for a splash of privacy.

In the glove compartment, next to the Glock 23, was a plastic sandwich bag. He cuffed the bag of exotic and twisted a blunt that resembled the shape of a baseball bat. After sparking the fat end, he took a long, lung-filling toke from it. Good weed always helped clear his mind and he was thankful that this batch was some of the best.

Eight seconds later he coughed up a thick ball of blue smoke. A sense of euphoria rolled through his body, along with the feeling of lightheadedness. Then he imagined a rapid concussion of fireworks going off. Weird.

Pop . . . Pop . . . Pop . . .

This was a sound he knew; the fireworks. This shit is better than I thought. He held the burning blunt up to his face. Gazing at the fatty as if it were a bar of gold spun from straw.

That's when it hit him.

Pow . . . Pow . . . Pow . . .

"Oh shit!"

A shard of glass from the blown-out rear window. It was turning out that the fireworks weren't even fireworks.

Pop! Pop! Pop!

They were gunshots. "What the fuc—"

A couple of copper slugs sparked off the trunk of the car. Before Lynx could react, two more slammed into the headrest of the passenger side. A fourth hammered into the rearview mirror, prying it away from the windshield. Ducking his head before slamming the car in gear, Lynx had no idea who was doing the shooting, or if it was more than one person. But as the storm of bullets continued to rain down on the car, he knew if he didn't break camp it wouldn't matter.

The barrage was coming from behind him. The same direction he'd driven from. That meant at least one thing was in his favor. His car was pointed in the opposite direction.

Wasting no more time, he punched the Audi's R-8 gas pedal and yanked the wheel and put the high-performance vehicle to the test. The Audi fishtailed into an acute left turn like a scared horse out of a starting shoot. He had no intentions of allowing a dilapidated car wash to become his makeshift mausoleum.

Not today.

The bullet-ridden Audi and his pounding heart raced along Charles Street for a few blocks, then turned along a main intersection, him wishing and hoping like hell this wasn't going to land him in a dead end. He drove for five or ten minutes before either of them slowed down. Lynx checked the rearview to see if anyone was behind him, but the mirror was laying on the floor, halfway beneath the passenger seat.

Shit, he couldn't blame the thing for hiding. If he hadn't had to drive, he probably would've ducked under the seat also. He used the mirror on the side to survey tail. He exhaled when he didn't see anyone following him. No longer under the immediate threat of gunfire, Lynx reflected on all the craziness.

Somebody snatched Nya.

He gets locked up for assaulting a police officer when reporting it.

Now somebody was trying to kill him.

Oh! And let's not forget the fifty Gs he lost on the game.

The day couldn't go any more wrong.

Okay, could it?

A searing pain shot through his arm when he tried to fish the phone from his pocket. He'd been so hopped up on adrenaline and fear, he'd failed to notice the blood on his shirtsleeve. A bullet had ripped through his right bicep. He tried moving the arm again. It hurt like hell, but cooperated. Thank God it wasn't worse, it was just a flesh wound.

Managing to finagle the phone from his pants without too much pain, he thumbed one of the preset numbers in his favorites.

"About time your ass called, where are you?" He could hear it in her voice, and she was pissed.

"Try to calm down, baby. I know this isn't easy, but it's going to be okay."

"How the hell is it going to be okay, Lynx? My fucking daughter is missing and we don't have the money to go get her?"

"How much is it?"

"Half a million."

"What you got in your stash?" he asked.

"There is no stash—I told you. I have been moving money from my stash to float my business, and when I checked the personal account there is a lot of money that can't be accounted for."

He paused, knowing she wanted an explanation and he felt less than that he was busted. He would have to admit to her that the gambling is more out of control than he'd ever wanted to admit. The truth of the matter, Lynx used to have a lot of money. He'd could win big, because he'd bet big. However, his luck hadn't been the best over the past couple of years and with him not making money hand over foot like he used to, his gambling turned to excessive and his bets got more desperate, digging him deeper and deeper into the hole. He hated to disappoint his wife but he had to tell the truth. "We gonna talk about it, just real bad investments, baby, but I promise I'm going to get it back." He was dumbfounded because he thought his wife was in a better situation financially.

"I'm gonna get our baby back," he said.

"How?" she screamed. "With no money?" He knew she wanted to believe in him but the circumstances were telling her something else.

"Listen, baby, it's going to be okay. I promise you!" He felt bad and was angry with himself mainly but also just at the overall situation. He didn't know how to react really.

"I don't think so. It's hard to be optimistic at a time like this."

Lynx could hear it in his wife's voice. She was about to break down. "Have some faith in me." He tried to convince her although he had no idea how he was going to make this entire situation right.

"And, oh, I almost forgot to tell you that your mistress and your son is here, homeless. So you tell me, how in the hell is this going to be okay?"

Before he could speak, she continued.

"Her and your son. And when were you planning to tell me about your secret family? This double life you are living?"

"Oh shit," he said to himself with a lump in his throat. He

knew one day things would hit the fan, just not this day. "What?" he asked, totally caught off guard.

"You heard me. I said Calliope and lil' Junior are here."

"Calm down."

"Calm down?"

"Yeah," he said, then it hit him that shit had really hit the fan at his house. "Calliope is there now?"

"Yup," Bambi said.

Though he had been shot at, and could've almost died, he was still calm. But knowing that two of the most important women in his life had been sitting eye to eye and the two worlds had collided, he could have shit a brick, and balls of perspiration were all across his face.

Just when he thought his day couldn't get any worse, now this double life that he'd been living had finally come to light. He thought about how true that saying was: what goes on in the dark always comes to the light. He tried to think if there was a time before when he felt like he had been boxed in any tighter. And the answer was no. This was the first time he didn't know how to handle himself in such a tight situation. So he did what first came to mind.

"Look, how about this . . . I haven't had the best day either, motherfuckers just shot at me. Trying to kill me, gunning me down. I just got shot and shit. So, I need to lay low, and try to figure out who is trying to kill me. So, you and Calliope gotta put y'alls head together and try to figure this shit out. Trust me, y'all resourceful as shit. Y'all basically on y'all own until I figure out who in the hell trying to kill me." And just like that he disconnected the phone.

36

The past ten hours of questions, answers, and soul searching amazingly created an odd closeness between Calliope and Bambi with Lynx being the common denominator in the duplicitous equation.

Ruby made breakfast: bacon, eggs, and hash browns. Seemingly oblivious to the gravity of the situation, Lynx Junior (looking just like his no-good daddy) was the only person in the house who got a wink of sleep. When he woke, he ate a few eggs and asked if he could play with Bambi's black cat Lucky. That was pretty much the only thing that could occupy him. Everything else was made for a princess—there were no monster trucks, trains, or planes around.

Burdened with her own problems, Bambi's first instinct was to tell this husband-stealing bitch to get the fuck out of her house. But after hearing Calliope's story, Bambi saw her in a different light. They both had been played—Bambi and Calliope—and since confronting Lynx on the phone, he showed just how much of a snake and coward he was by refusing to answer another one of their calls after he hung up. They tried everything they could to get his cheating, bitch-ass on the phone—different numbers and text messages. But Lynx had gone completely off the grid. His actions stated the obvious: Fuck Nya! Fuck Calliope! Fuck Lynx Junior! And Fuck her!

After getting the e-mail asking for the money in return for Nya, Bambi had checked the balance of their joint savings account, a goose egg. The little more than a hundred grand that should've been there was gone. No doubt another casualty of Lynx's gambling. *Who was this dude?* Besides one hella an actor, Bambi thought, while pushing the bacon around on her plate.

Basically a one-night stand. That was how Calliope described the genesis of their deceptive relationship. She'd been emotionally frazzled by her brother's death and hell-bent on making someone pay for it. That was the reason she was in Magic City Casino that day looking for Jiggilo.

Then Lynx came along talking about how she'd been his good-luck charm, and how he needed to return the favor to keep all things right with nature and the gambling gods. In other words, Lynx put the moves on her, taking straight advantage of Calliope's vulnerable condition.

"The shopping spree and dinner," he'd offered. "You look like you could use a bit of cheering up." She couldn't hide the distress she was feeling, the hurt, the loss. The brief interruption by Lynx had allowed her a moment to rethink what she'd been planning to do. How smart would it be to shoot a man in the middle of a crowded casino? And how would going to jail for the rest of her life help Compton? It wouldn't. Therefore, she needed to be wiser. A better time would present a better opportunity.

To Lynx, she'd said, "I'll take you up on that offer." Lynx did everything he said he would do and more. The night ended up with what was supposed to have been one night of sensual sin, except the condom broke and she got pregnant.

Hearing Calliope talk about how she met Lynx dredged up a lot of old memories for Bambi. Bambi would never admit it, but in a weird way, she felt a tinge of jealousy toward Calliope. Calliope had something from Lynx that she didn't and could never have. Because Bambi couldn't conceive children, Nya had been adopted, something almost no one besides close family knew about. Yet Bambi could not have loved Nya any more if she had come out of her own womb. She thought Lynx felt the same way. Now she wasn't sure.

To no one in particular, Bambi blurted out, "Fuck Lynx! I have to come up with that five hundred thousand, no ifs, ands, or buts about it." The people who had taken Nya were serious. What if the reason they tried to snatch Calliope's son was because they somehow figured out that Nya wasn't Lynx's child by blood? And now she is no good to them? What if they didn't think it was worth the trouble keeping Nya alive?

Ruby cleared the table. No one was eating anyway.

"I'll try to help any way I can." Calliope's phone rang just when she was about to clarify that she was talking about helping with the money, not the dishes. "I think I should take this," she said.

Bambi couldn't help but wonder who the call was from.

"Hello?"

Calliope hadn't spoken to the other person on the other end of the phone in a while. "Where are you?" Jean asked.

"None of your business" is what she wanted to say. Instead she asked, "Why?"

"Because you may be in serious trouble."

"This isn't a good time for riddles, Jean. If you have something to tell me, tell me."

Bambi had thought that maybe it was Lynx on the other end of the phone! But that notion had been nixed when Calliope used the name Jean. To Calliope, Jean sounded both sincere and contrite when he said, "I never meant you any harm. However"—Jean changed the subject before it really began—"I didn't call to regurgitate our past."

But the past always somehow has a hand in the present. And this time was no different, Calliope would soon find out.

Jean continued, "That cat you moved out of town to Virginia with—Lynx, right? People are looking for him."

Strange, Calliope thought. She'd never told Jean that she was leaving Miami or with Lynx. When she found out she was pregnant, she told Lynx and he convinced her to leave. She needed a fresh start. Once she got the wrongful-death-lawsuit money from the city, she just up and left.

"How do you know I moved away with Lynx?"

"You should know—knowing things keep me ahead of the game. To be aware is to be alive," Jean philosophically quoted. "I think I should've been that boy's daddy," he reminded her, and then changed the subject. "Anyway, dude is in bad graces with some even badder people."

Tell me something I don't know.

Jean went on to inform Calliope that Lynx owed a lot of bread to a ruthless clique of people. The type of folks that had no compunctions with kidnapping kids and using them as collateral. The lion's share of what Jean had told her, Calliope had already figured out, but not all of it. Jean said, "He owe the money to a band of crazy-ass Russians."

The past always somehow has a hand in the present.

"Not just any crazy Russians," Jean said. "These are the same guys that almost killed you back in the day."

What the fuck . . .

"The ones that had killed the cop, like he was nothing, in cold blood," Calliope remembered. How could she forget?

"You mean Mikile?"

This was bizarre for Calliope to wrap her mind around. "Mikile and the man in the closet is trying to take my baby? And have already taken Bambi's little girl?"

"Whoa! I'm just telling you what the streets are telling me. And I don't even know anyone named Bambi. I just wanted you to know what the score was. The game can be tricky."

Jean didn't have any more to tell her, nor did he offer any solutions; so Calliope ended the conversation there.

"No hard feelings," Jean had said before she killed the line.

Bambi, stricken with grief, said, "What were you saying about some Russian that may have taken Nya?" Her eyes were red and puffy.

The quick version was all Calliope managed to explain before she felt compelled to hug Lynx Junior. She jumped from the kitchen table and headed to the screened-in porch, where he was playing with Bambi's cat. But when she got there she didn't see him. Smeared on the floor was something that looked like blood.

Calliope screamed as loud as she had ever screamed in her life, *"Noooo!"*

Bambi and Ruby came to see what had rattled her.

The blood Calliope had seen had belonged to the cat. Lucky was dead. Someone had chopped the poor feline's head off. Lucky was the first present that Lynx had ever given to Bambi. She had loved him like a member of the family. It seemed symbolic of her and Lynx's relationship being dead as well.

And to make matters worse, Lynx, Jr. was gone.

Vanished.

Knowing what Calliope was feeling firsthand, Bambi put her arms around her. Calliope went limp and wouldn't or couldn't stop balling with tears. It took all of Bambi's strength to keep Calliope from collapsing to the ground, trying to control her. Bambi said, "We are gonna get through this." But it didn't do much good. Her own heart was too weak to strengthen another's. Ruby joined them.

They all in some form or another shared the same single thought: *Why was this happening?*

Two minutes passed . . . another three minutes, tops, before they pulled it together.

"Okay," Bambi said, pulling away from the group hug. "This isn't going to get Nya or Lynx Junior back." The name Lynx Junior felt alien rolling off of her tongue. "This isn't the time to be crying like little bitches. We need to tighten up and figure out a plan of action." Bambi placed her hand on Calliope's shoulders. "Okay?"

Calliope sniffled and nodded. "I know one person that may be able to help."

The words came out muffled.

"That's what I'm talking about. Any action beats no action."

"It's my Big Spender. He was one of my old customers from when I was dancing. He holds a lot of power and has unlimited bank."

Funny, Bambi thought. Calliope didn't think about Mr. Money Bags until her child got taken.

As she could read Bambi's mind, Calliope said, "I was gonna reach out to him for you before I got the call from Jean."

Bambi felt a pea of guilt. Calliope had mentioned helping to get the money before her phone rang. "Then let's not waste any more time. What's this dude's name?"

No way could Bambi have been prepared for all of this. She and Calliope' worlds would be even more intertwined.

"His name is Lou, short for Lootchee."

Bambi used to date a guy name Lootchee back before she met Lynx. He was caked up and from Texas. What were the odds of there being two Lootchees in the world. Bambi and *her* Lootchee had split on bad terms. When she found out that dude had been transporting drugs through the mail using her name— lots of drugs—Bambi turned the tables on who was gaming who. She took all of Lootchee's stash and made him think that all the drugs were confiscated by the Feds. With wind that the Feds were on his trail, Lootchee wasted no time relocating to

Mexico. While down there he met a chick name Unique that was selling pussy for a Mexican pimp. Unique's boyfriend—on some get-back shit—had sold her to the pimp for a kilo of coke, a chicken, and donkey, leaving Unique to work the debt off to pay for her freedom.

Lootchee fell in love with Unique and her state-of-the-art blow-job talents, and he was willing to spend the rest of his life in Mexico with her until he seen Bambi on BET promoting a million-dollar party-planning business. That's when he knew he had been tricked and vowed to make Bambi pay and this was the man that Calliope now wanted to call for help! *The past always somehow has its hands in the present,* Bambi thought.

"If you think he can help . . . call him," Bambi said with her heart in her stomach. She knew that she'd have to pay the price for double-crossing Lootchee, but if he was willing to get their kids back, then she'd sacrifice herself.

Calliope dialed the number. Someone answered. "Hello, Lou."

It was him.

"This is Calliope. . . . Lootchee, I need your help."

37

Mikile stood across the street from Bambi's house leaning on a late-model 750 BMW. Calliope made her way across the street, as Ruby watched at the door with pistol cocked. "Long time no see. You've grown to be a beautiful lady. I thought you were pretty back then, but," he whistled and nodded as he looked her over. "You have turned into quite a knockout."

She couldn't even make herself say thank you. She wanted to pull out the hunter's knife in her pocket so badly and stab him or cut his throat. But she didn't, because he had her baby. But what she did do was cut right through the small talk, "What is it that you want? And why the fuck would you take my baby?"

"It's simple, baby. It's collateral."

"You are going to get your money, one way or the other," she bluntly told him as convincingly as she knew how.

"No, it's more to it than the money."

"What do you mean?"

"You owe me."

"I owe you?" she questioned.

"Yes, because I liked you, I spared you many years ago." He threw his hands up. "Now you owe me for giving you life, and not taking it."

"You getting the money. Or is it your people aren't going to break you off?"

He ignored her question, and got straight to the point. "The same way Rusty used you. I need you to provide that same service to me."

She was surprised. "What? I don't do that anymore."

"You want to see your son alive again, don't you? And especially if you want him to be Junior and not Genie, then you will make your services available to me."

"What?" She sucked her teeth and said in the nastiest disposition she could without offending him.

"You will bring your baby father out of hiding and then we will take care of him."

"Hell, if I knew where he was at—"

He cut her off with a chuckle. "You are one crafty bitch. But you will do what you have to do to take care of that boy of yours . . . the same way you did to take care of your brother. Right?"

The mere mention of Compton by Mikile pissed her off. But she nodded and tried to stay focused on the only thing that really mattered, the kids.

"What about the little girl?"

Mikile looked confused. "Little girl?" he questioned. "We don't have no girl, only da boy."

Where the hell was Nya? Who in the hell had her? And what

the hell were they going to do to get up the cash they needed? How in the hell would she get Lynx out of hiding? Shit just got so real in the realest way! The one thing they knew was to never underestimate a mother's love, a woman's scorn, and three bad bitches and Girl Power!

31901064316898

CPSIA information can be obtained
at www.ICGtesting.com
Printed in the USA
LVHW041626280219
609077LV00002B/289/P